Temptation Trail

Max Quinn stood alone in the street of Sundance, Wyoming. Before him, arranged in a well-spaced arc, stood three of the fastest gunmen he had ever faced. The small, psychotic one of the trio tittered briefly. 'Let's see if you're fast enough to deal with all three of us,' he gloated. Max should have heeded the warning vision that had come to him that night. He should have gone somewhere, anywhere, except to Sundance.

He tensed to draw, determined at least to die making the best effort of his life.

Temptation Trail

Billy Hall

A Black Horse Western

ROBERT HALE · LONDON

ISBN 978-0-7090-8554-6

Robert Hale Limited
Clerkenwell House
Clerkenwell Green
London EC1R 0HT

www.halebooks.com

Typeset by
Derek Doyle & Associates, Shaw Heath
Printed and bound in Great Britain by
Antony Rowe Limited, Wiltshire

CHAPTER 1

His sharp intake of breath was the only sound. In all the vast expanse of the universe, no other sound intruded. Nothing else existed. None else inhabited.

His eyes opened wide. The pupils dilated at the vision before him.

A woman stood at the edge of his campsite. It didn't even occur to him to wonder how she had gotten there. The full moon bathed her in gentle light, illuminating every exquisite feature.

No longing dream of lonely nights on the trail could ever have conjured so perfect an image. To say she was beautiful would be like calling one's mother 'some relative'. Her semblance reached so far beyond what beauty describes as to make the very word itself seem mundane, meaningless.

She was stroking her long, black hair with a brush that caught and reflected bits and pieces of the moon's rays. Those same rays shimmered and danced in the smooth, rippling waves of her radiant locks. Each hair seemed alive in and of itself, flirting with other strands in a seductive, fluid dance. Bits of stardust flew from each motion, fading away into the soft magic of the night. Moonlight on a gently rolling sea could not have been more liquid, more entrancing.

The cascading waves of hair framed a face of the most delicate beauty he had ever beheld. Dark eyes glistened beneath long lashes, curled upward as if to frame and accent the deep pools of mystery below them. A small nose, lifted ever so slightly just at the end, formed an exclamation point above more inviting lips than his wildest dreams could ever have invented. Full, ripe, open just slightly to show an even row of glistening white teeth, their flawless invitation made him ache physically. Every fiber of his being was drawn to those lips. He could almost feel his own touch them, press against them, thrill at their response to his own.

Her lightly bronzed skin seemed to absorb the soft rays of moonlight, spreading the fire of its glow beneath the skin. The moon's glow and her own seemed to be released and absorbed in a constant exchange of beauty that left both somehow greater, and diminished neither.

She laid the brush on the fallen tree upon which she sat, and stood as he approached. She was shorter than he by six inches. Her hands and feet were slender, dainty, sparkling clean. The white linen gown flowimg from her shoulders seemed at once to mask the flawlessness of her form at the same time it accented every curve, every feature. It glowed in the

6

reflected moonlight almost as if it were as alive as her skin. It rippled and flowed around her of its own volition. It clung momentarily to each segment of the entrancing body within it. It seemed to deliberately accent for an instant the perfect roundness of a breast, then the flat softness of the stomach. It moved to the full sway of the hips, to the lines of superbly shaped legs, then back again to the rise of shoulders. The shape of the gown incessantly changed in the light breeze. It constantly caressed her, emphasizing every feature of the divine form it covered.

He was suddenly aware of her contrast with his own appearance. Rough cut at best, he felt the three days' growth of beard that stubbled his jaw and face. His eyes were drawn to the almost sterile pink perfection of her fingernails. He saw in his mind the ragged ends of his own, dirt beneath making them dark and ugly.

The hypnotic flowing of her stunningly white gown contrasted with the faded coarseness of his wool flannel shirt and corduroy trousers. He hadn't changed either one in more than a week. Stale sweat permeated those clothes. The odor of his own body telegraphed the knowledge that he had to be unbearably repulsive.

The worn holster that held the Colt .45, tied low on his hip, felt suddenly too heavy to wear, too out of place in her presence. It was too much an instrument of death to be here in the presence of the life and love that her whole being exuded. Every facet of his being stood in stark and utter contrast to her perfection.

7

His fears and reticence, however, were immediately allayed. It startled, then confused, then elated him that her response was exactly opposite from what he was convinced it must be.

As her eyes fell on him they lit up with an ineffable joy that radiated into the deepest core of his being. Her maddeningly inviting lips opened in a broad smile of welcome. She radiated not just acceptance of everything he was, but inexpressible love and delight. Greater joy than he had ever experienced welled up within him, threatening to overwhelm him in a rising tide of pure delight.

As if in a trance, he walked forward until he was ten feet in front of her, then stopped. A faint wisp of some mysterious perfume wafted past him on the breeze. His eyes were drawn to her hair, from where that entrancing essence emanated. He was suddenly obsessed with an all but irresistible urge to bury his face in those silken tresses. He wanted to breath that soft perfume, to be borne on the wings of its bouquet, carried far away to some ecstatic place where none but angels dwell.

He knew he was being rude. He couldn't help himself. He stared openly, hungrily. However much he tried, he could not stop his eyes from roving up and down the vision of unblemished beauty before him. His gaze rested for an instant on each point of perfection, then moved quickly on, as if desperate to sate every starved sense of his being.

He couldn't even close his mouth, though he knew he gaped, slack jawed at her transcendent beauty.

All sense of his own inadequacy, ineptness, uncleanness was banished instantly and completely by her radiant smile, by the dancing eyes of her welcome, by the love that reached out from her breast to envelop him. She lifted her arms to him, walking forward to meet him. As she did, ebony hair and snowy gown flowed outward in the breeze behind her, driving the last breath from his lungs, and the last thread of resistance from his mind.

Even so, something stopped him, just before their arms enveloped each other. He hesitated, pulled back away. Unaware of any reason to do so, he fought desperately against every yearning instinct of his body.

Her expression did not change. She did not seem to notice. She did not, however, wrap her arms around him. Instead, she reached out one of the exquisitely formed hands and laid it on his left wrist, extended toward her.

Reality shifted with stunning abruptness. Instead of the gentle glow of a lover's touch that he antici-pated, her fingers wrapped around his wrist with an iron grip. Fierce cold, rather than warmth, radiated from the touch. Burning cold, such as he had never felt, stabbed through his arm. It flowed upward through his arm, into his shoulder.

Frigid tentacles knifed through him, encasing his chest and lungs in a frosty vise. Bitingly cold fingers reached to wrap around his heart, to squeeze it in their freezing grip.

The ivory gleam of her teeth gripped his gaze. The

smile was still there, but the luscious fullness of lips had given way to the mindless ferocity of clenched teeth. If he could have torn his eyes from the teeth, he was sure they would be surrounded by a faceless skull, fixed in the macabre grin of death.

Stark terror flooded his mind, enveloping his senses, erasing all reason. He strained against the steely grip with which she held him. He tried to brace his other hand against her, but some unseen presence seemed to fend it away. He jerked and wrenched, fighting to wrest his arm from that freezing embrace.

He willed the imprisoned arm to pull away, but it was past responding to his will. It remained rigid, unresponsive, serving only as a fixed and frozen conduit for the frigid tide of death flowing through it to the rest of his body.

He screamed 'No!' at the top of his voice.

He twisted his body away from her with every ounce of rapidly diminishing strength, flinging himself backward.

Abruptly, inexplicably, she was gone.

Eyes cast wildly about. He stood at the edge of his campsite, wrapped in one torn and twisted blanket of his bedroll. He jerked his left arm frantically to free it from the ensnaring folds of cloth.

Around him, no sound disturbed the serenity of the glade. Behind him, the sheer wall of rock rose fifty feet into the moonlight. Before him, the thick bramble of bushes that stretched away for a hundred yards in a half circle gave no evidence of any intruder.

From the corner of his eye he saw his picketed horse, watching him curiously, wondering momentarily at the sudden explosion of sound from his master. After a moment, the chestnut gelding dropped his head and resumed cropping the lush grass.

His eyes darted this way and that, battling the panic that surged within him. He fought to bring his breathing under control, to steady its ragged gasps and gulps.

He slowly sank down against the rough wall of rock, folding his knees up to his chest. He clutched the ripped and tattered blanket closely around himself, willing the violent tremors to cease their racking of his body.

He had faced death many times. He had never felt its fear before. Not like this. And he didn't even know what 'this' was.

Max Quinn told himself it was just a dream. Even as he did so, he knew better. It was more than a dream. Much more. He just didn't know how much more.

CHAPTER 2

He eased the Colt .45 in its holster. His right hand remained resting on his thigh, inches from the gun.

Restless eyes scanned the main street of Sundance, Wyoming. On the edges of town, several tents served as saloons and various temporary businesses. That the gold rush into the neighboring Black Hills of Dakota Territory had spilled over here was immediately obvious.

In contrast to the hastily erected tents, sturdy buildings made up most of the main street. Several boasted high façades, with carefully lettered signs announcing their wares:

MERCANTILE & DRY GOODS.

HARDWARE & SUPPLIES.

GUNS BOUGHT, SOLD & REPAIRED.

DOTTIE'S MILLINERY & LACE GOODS.

The unmistakable ring of a blacksmith's hammer against the anvil sent a rhythmic heartbeat of a busy town along its store fronts.

In almost the exact center of the business district

a massive, two-story edifice loomed above its neigh-bors. A sign that could be read for a quarter of a mile announced, MCMASTER'S GOOD TIMES, in red block letters. Below that its legend announced, Liquor, Gaming, & Pleasure Palace.

Next to the more crude construction of the rest of the businesses, it truly emulated the appearance of a palace.

Its size afforded room for a row of hitching rails. At either end of the porch that fronted the entire building, a small sign announced, Corral & feed available in back.

The only structure in town that rivaled it was across the street, half a block further along. It, too, was a two-story structure, with a veranda across the front, affording a balcony for each of the rooms on the second floor, as well as shielding the board side-walk from inclement weather. Its sign boasted, in black letters, WALTMAN'S SALOON & GAMING. On the line below it boasted, Fair Priced Liquor and Honest Games.

'Now there's a slap in the face at someone,' Max muttered.

He rode slowly the length of the business district, until its stores gave way to residences and side streets. Riding to the nearest alley, he reversed his direction. He rode the length of the town, back the way he had come, carefully examining all the businesses from the rear.

It was easy to spot McMaster's, even from the back. Behind the two-story building a large corral was furnished with feed bunks at regular intervals. A grain bin and a small haystack provided feed for any mounts left in the corral. Both were available, apparently, without charge. More than a dozen horses were secured by feed bunks. Half-a-dozen others were untethered, left to help themselves to feed provided for the others.

A hand pump provided well water for a tank that protruded into the corral. It was filled with water.

'At least he takes care of his customers' horses,' Max approved.

When he had ridden the length of the town behind the businesses on that side of its main street, he repeated the action behind the businesses on the other side of the street.

Emerging again where the residential district began, he retraced his earlier path down the main street. He dismounted in front of McMaster's. Tying his horse loosely at one of the less crowded rails, he walked through the batwing doors.

The inside of the saloon was impressive, to say the least.

A huge bar of polished mahogany ran the length of one end of the room. The wall behind it was almost entirely mirror, except for the spot in the exact center. There, a bigger-than-life painting of a well-endowed, naked woman, lying indolently on luxurious bedding, provided irresistible allure to lonesome cowboys, prospectors, soldiers and drifters. It was lighted by twin chandeliers, making it the brightest spot in the establishment.

14

In addition to the bar, and the inevitable array of tables for groups of varying sizes to drink, gamble, or just visit, there was a large area reserved for serious gaming. Three separate roulette wheels ratcheted their spinning promise of sudden wealth, to the chorus of cries for the capricious ball to stop at some desperately desired spot.

Games of cards and dice, encompassing about every form of gambling Max knew, progressed at some point in the place.

Amongst it all, a substantial number of scantily clad women moved among the patrons, openly flirting with any man who made eye contact.

As he moved toward the bar, one of the patrons whispered something in the ear of one of them. She responded with a giggle that managed to sound delighted. She said, 'If you want that, cowboy, you need a bath first.'

'So where can I get a bath?'

She pointed to a door at the rear of the room. 'Right through there, cowboy. I'll be waiting when you're done.'

'What's your name?' he asked, rising hurriedly to comply.

'Just ask for Rosie if you don't see me,' she answered.

The cowboy, still grimy from weeks of lonely ranch life, nearly tripped across tables rushing to the bath and promised pleasures beyond.

Bet he ain't got a nickel of wages when he leaves here, Max thought.

He ordered a beer at the bar and paid for it, studying the room behind him in the surprisingly clean mirror.

As he sipped the cool liquid, he noticed for the first time a row of tables that sat empty, forming a line almost straight across the saloon section of the room. When one of the three bartenders had an idle moment, he asked, 'Why's the row of tables empty?'

The bartender shrugged. 'Sorta no-man's-land.'

'No-man's-land? There a war goin' on?'

He shook his head. 'Nah. Nothin' like that. Well, not open-like, anyway. Hands that ride for the big ranches just don't 'sociate much with the small ranchers and homesteaders.'

Max lifted his eyebrows. 'What about folks that're neither?'

The bartender shrugged again. 'They either fit in with one group or the other. Or else they stand at the bar like you're a-doin'.'

Max started to ask a further question, but a growing commotion caught his attention. He moved away from the bar to have a clearer look.

A cowboy, obviously dressed in his best go-to-town clothes, was being confronted by a man nearly twice his size. Behind the big man, three others ranged in obvious support.

'Two-bit cowboys hadn't oughta have fancy watches in their vest like that, that's all I'm sayin'.'

'Why not?' the cowboy demanded.

'Ain't fittin', that's all. Ain't no way you can make enough honest money to buy a fancy watch and fob like that there.'

'I didn't buy it; it was my grandfather's.'

'Is that so?' demanded the antagonist. 'Then I bet there ain't nothin' you'd not do to keep it, huh?'

With astonishing speed, his hand shot out and grabbed the ornate gold fob that draped across the front of the cowboy's vest. He jerked the watch from its pocket, breaking the fob.

The cowboy's hand dropped instantly to his gun, but so did the hands of all three of the antagonist's friends. The cowboy hesitated.

His assailant laughed roughly. 'Sure is a fine watch,' he chortled, eyeing the timepiece admiringly. 'If you want it back, go get it.'

With that he tossed the watch into the nearest spittoon. It landed with a splash that verified the contents of the brass container were considerable.

'Dig it out,' the big man demanded.

The cowboy's eyes burned bright with helpless anger. His hand curled just above his gun butt. Just when it appeared that he would be foolish enough to take on all four of the rowdies, even at the expense of his life, Max stepped forward.

He stepped across between the two men, sweeping his foot across the spot where the big man stood. It swept his feet out from under him, sprawling him with his face almost against the spittoon. 'Why don't you dig it out?' Max asked in a deceptively soft voice.

The big man cursed and sprang to his feet. He no sooner reached his feet than he sprawled on to the floor again. A swiftly rising welt along the side of his head marked where Max's gun barrel had smashed against his skull.

Before the big man hit the floor the second time, that gun was leveled on the three friends. Almost as one they swallowed hard, their smiles gone, eyes wide with surprise.

Without taking his eyes from the trio, Max addressed the cowboy, frozen in his tracks as immovable as the other three. 'Best fetch your watch, cowboy.'

The words ripped the invisible restraints from the young man. A huge grin spread across his face. He strode over to the spittoon, picked it up, and dumped its contents, watch and all, on the head of the unconscious bully. Then he jerked the man's shirt-tail out of his trousers. Using it, he dragged the dripping timepiece across the man's slightly parted lips. 'Have a taste of your own medicine, when you wake up,' he grinned.

Then he carefully cleaned the watch with the man's shirt. When he was finished, he replaced the watch in his vest pocket and stood up. He drew his own gun and took his place beside Max. Eyeing the cowed trio, he asked, 'Can I shoot me one or two of 'em?'

'The boss ain't gonna like that,' the bartender offered. 'He don't like trouble inside here.'

Ignoring him, Max addressed the cowboy. 'Let's clear out,' he ordered.

Together the two backed out of the saloon together, eyes darting in all directions. As they exited the batwing doors, the big man was just beginning to stir. He wiped a hand across his mouth, then spit in disgust. They didn't stick around to watch any more.

'Your horse out here?' Max queried.

'Right over there.'

'Best get mounted up. Those boys might come out shooting any time.'

'Odds ain't so bad now, though,' the cowboy grinned.

In spite of his bravado, he walked quickly to his horse and stepped into the saddle.

When they were safely away from the town, the cowboy addressed his rescuer. 'By the way, I'm Champ Haggler. Thanks for buying in, back there.'

He stuck out his hand. Max took the hand and shook it. 'Max Quinn. They friends of yours, are they?'

Champ's grin, that seemed to spring easily to his face, came again. 'Naw. Some of the hired toughs the small ranchers have brought in. They're always looking for trouble.'

'Small ranchers hiring fighters,' Max mused. 'Does sound like trouble.'

'Gonna be, that's for sure,' Champ agreed.

'I take it you work for one of the big spreads.'

'Yup. Triangle, right now. I usually work either for them or Bald Mountain, or maybe the Mill Iron. You lookin' for work?'

'Might be,' Max evaded. 'Triangle a good place to work?'

'Always has been,' Champ qualified. 'None of 'em

19

are as good as they used to be. Too much stuff in the air, these days. Everybody's on edge. Some of the smaller guys are selling out and leaving the country. Or just disappearing. Homesteaders, too. Some aim to tough it out.'

'Perfect recipe for a range war,' Max observed.

'So far it ain't come to that. Sure hope it don't. Ridin' out to the ranch with me?'

Max shook his head. 'No, I 'spect not tonight. Might ride out later. I ain't got my fill of town yet.'

Champ eyed him warily. 'You might be a bit careful, ridin' back into Sundance. There's four fellas there that might just love to have another go at you.'

'I'll watch my back,' Max assured him. 'Take care.'

Champ nodded. 'You too. When you're ready to get to work, come on out. I'll put in a good word for you with the foreman.'

'Thanks,' Max offered as he reined his horse around and headed back toward Sundance.

CHAPTER 3

'Please move out of my way, and leave me alone!'

The combination of anger and fear in the woman's voice brought Max up short.

Splashes of light from windows and doors offered meager illumination. He crossed Sundance's main street swiftly, moving toward the sound.

A man's voice responded to the woman's demand, but he could not hear what was said. He could certainly hear her retort.

'Get your hands off me and get out of my way. I am not one of the saloon girls!'

The man's voice chuckled softly. Max was close enough to hear the man's softer voice as he said, 'That's what I like, honey. A little fire. You're prettier'n a picture, too.'

'Get away from me!'

In the shadows at the front of a store, closed for the evening, Max made out the figure of a woman, backed into a corner by that store's front door. Facing her, a cowboy leaned against the store's front wall. His arm effectively blocked her only direction of escape.

'Now stop pretendin' you don't want me, honey,' the man's voice teased. 'You'n me are gonna have a real fun time right over there on the ground. I ain't had me a woman in a long time.'

Max grabbed the cowboy by the back of his shirt collar. He jerked him away from the woman, sending him staggering into the darkened street.

'The lady asked you to leave her alone,' Max said affably. 'There's plenty of the kind of girls you're looking for at the saloon.'

The cowboy fought to maintain his balance for an instant before he righted himself. Even in the darkness Max could see the anger in his stance. His voice echoed the belligerence. 'Who're you?' he demanded.

'Doesn't matter,' Max dismissed the question. 'You just made a mistake, friend. The lady isn't interested. You'd best head back over to the saloon.'

The cowpoke walked back up to face Max. 'I don't need you to tell me where to go,' he insisted. 'Or who to talk to neither. Get outa here and mind your own business.'

'Wrong idea.' Max's voice grew flatter, its edges hard with warning. 'You've had a drink or two too many to think straight.'

The cowhand drew himself up to full height. 'Drunk or sober, I can think straight, shoot straight and dang sure put an end to your meddlin',' he threatened.

As he finished the slurred speech, his hand lifted

from his holster, his gun firmly and steadily gripped. In spite of his state of intoxication, he was surprisingly fast.

Max's fist was even faster. It slammed into the young man's chin with sledgehammer force. It made a 'chunk' sound as it connected. The cowboy sprawled backward into the street. He lay spread-eagled, unmoving. The gun flew from his hand and landed two feet away from his outstretched hand.

Max stepped forward and picked up the sidearm. He thumbed the cartridges out of the cylinder and dropped them in his pocket. Then he replaced the empty weapon in its holster. Only then did he turn his attention to the woman.

Turning, he removed his hat and addressed her. 'Are you all right, ma'am?'

She stood where she had been, riveted to the corner by the store's front door. Her posture radiated fear, but her voice was surprisingly strong and steady. 'I am quite fine. Thank you. I owe you three thanks, I believe.'

Confusion was obvious in his voice. 'Three thanks?'

She nodded. She finally stepped away from the wall she had been transfixed against. 'Quite,' she repeated. 'Thank you for coming to my aid. Thank you for disposing of the young man. And thank you for not killing him.'

'He didn't need killing,' Max observed. 'He's just had a snootful of rotgut, after being lonesome too long.'

23

'Nevertheless,' she argued, 'it would have been easy to justify killing him when he pulled his gun. He might have killed you. It would have been clearly self-defense.'

'He was too drunk to be that much of a threat.'

'He appeared extremely fast with that gun, to me.'

'Faster'n I expected, all right,' he admitted. 'Still, not near that fast.'

Even in the darkness he could feel her appraising look. 'Are you so much faster that his speed was no threat to you?'

'Well, yes, ma'am.'

'Are you a gunfighter?'

'No, ma'am. Just another out of work cowpoke.'

'You're not a lawman, then?'

He grinned. 'Don't see any badge, do you?'

'It's much too dark to be sure.'

'Much too dark for a lady to be walking alone on the street, too.'

Silence hung thickly for several seconds. It was she who broke it. 'I was about to retort rather automatically that I am perfectly capable of taking care of myself, but I'm afraid that bit of bravado would sound rather foolish just now, wouldn't it?'

He chuckled. 'Yes, ma'am, it would. May I walk you home, in case there is more than one misguided cowboy lurking about?'

'Lurking!' she marveled, a teasing lilt suddenly invading her voice. 'I haven't heard that word used in Sundance often.'

'Would skulking perhaps be more apropos?'

24

She giggled unexpectedly. 'My! It's even an educated white knight who has come to my rescue.'

'Pretty dark to be very sure of the color, isn't it?'

She giggled again. 'Not even grimy around the collar, if I am any judge of voices,' she observed.

It was his turn to chuckle. 'It gets pretty grimy once in a while,' he admitted. 'Which way are you heading?'

'I don't remember giving you permission to walk me home,' she reminded him.

'Well, then, shall we start over? May I have the honor of walking you home?'

'I would be most happy for you to do so.'

'Then which way are we headed?' he placed heavy accent on the 'we'.

She giggled again. 'My house is about two blocks this way.'

'Then may I offer you my arm, madam?'

'Why, thank you, sir.'

The feeling the touch of her hand on his arm triggered in him was surprising. It left him momentarily speechless as they began to walk the way she had indicated. After a little way, he began to remember his manners. 'Oh, I should apologize. I didn't even introduce myself. I'm Max Quinn.'

'Maxwell Quinn,' she echoed.

'Now I haven't heard the full name since I left home. Sounds strange.'

'Do you have a middle name?'

'Not that I'll admit to.'

'How about one you don't like to admit?'

'Aw, I usually just tell people that ask that my folks were too poor to give me that many names.'

Laughter threatened to break the surface of her voice. 'But when people are too skeptical or too nosy to accept that, to what middle name do you admit?'

'Promise you won't laugh?'

'Promise.'

'Horatio.'

'Maxwell Horatio Quinn. That's a very distinguished name.'

His dry, flat-voiced response caught her completely off guard. 'With gilded edges all set about and proper scrolling on the large letters.'

The lilting melody of her laughter drifted across the darkened street. 'Red, of course, on a white background.'

'Just like a circus wagon.'

'Or a medicine man's.'

'You haven't told me your name.'

She hesitated only an instant. 'My name is Dorothea Fancher. Dottie to my friends, which I guess you have earned the right to be considered.'

'Now there has to be a middle name in there, too.'

Again, she hesitated only briefly. 'Dorothea Marie Dixon Fancher.'

She could feel the instant distance between them, even though neither had moved from walking side by side, her hand resting lightly on his left arm. He gave voice to his instant conjecture. 'Fancher is your married name, I assume.'

'It is.'

Silence hung heavily as he tried to form an acceptable answer. He was troubled by the sudden sense of disappointment that threatened to overwhelm him. She eventually answered the question she knew he had to be wondering.

'No, my husband doesn't allow me to walk the streets alone. He is deceased.'

'I'm sorry,' was all he could think to say. He felt hypocritical even saying that. He wasn't a bit sorry. In fact, an ebullient joy bubbled up within him at her explanation. It was all he could do to resist shouting his sudden exultation into the night sky.

'It was almost two years ago,' she volunteered. 'That's when I moved into Sundance and opened up the shop.'

'Shop?'

'Oh, I'm sorry. I completely forgot I hadn't told you. I own Dottie's Millinery And Lace Goods. It's almost a block back from where you . . . rescued me.'

'Late closing up, tonight, huh?'

'Yes. I am almost always home before dark. Except in the wintertime, of course. It gets dark so early then.'

'Good idea to be off the streets before dark.' The observation seemed hollow, almost sanctimonious, even as he said it.

'It's usually not a problem. My shop is more than half a block this side of all the saloons and gambling places. Well, Waltman's is just barely half a block away, on the other side of the street, but it's not as bad as McMaster's.'

27

'McMaster's is quite a place,' he observed.

She did not answer immediately. When she did, her voice was edged with flint. 'Everything that man does is—' The sentence hung unfinished in the air.

'This is my house,' she announced.

They turned up a path that led to a low porch fronting a small, single-story house. 'Thank you very much for seeing me home.'

'Would you like me to wait here until you get a lamp lit?'

She hesitated only briefly. 'Yes. That would be very kind of you.'

She stepped inside, careful to not let the screen door bang. In a few seconds a match flared inside, then the soft glow of a kerosene lamp spilled out through the screen.

'Good night, Dorothea Marie Dixon Fancher,' he said through the door.

She opened the door and smiled at him. He could see her face for the first time. She was shockingly beautiful. 'Good night, Maxwell Horatio Quinn,' she responded.

Swallowing hard against the lump in his throat, Max turned and hurried back down the short path to the street. He was a dozen steps down the street before he heard the screen door close softly.

CHAPTER 4

He woke with a start. Before he realized he had been wakened, he was sitting bolt upright in the sagging bed. His .45 was in his hand. Alarms sounded deep in some corner of his brain that never slept.

His eyes darted to the straight-backed chair, propped with its back just under the doorknob. It was securely in place.

In the instant his eyes confirmed its protection, he realized he shouldn't be able to see it. He had been asleep only a couple hours. It should have been pitch dark.

Instead, the room was bathed in reddish light. It took another instant for the cobwebs of sleep to clear from his mind.

'Fire!' he breathed.

He lunged to the window, looking out from the second-story window. Fire was licking up the sides of Waltman's Saloon & Gambling Parlor.

He jerked his clothes on, noting the thunder of booted feet already trooping down the hotel steps.

He joined them in little over a minute, hurrying into the street.

Three bucket brigades were already forming, making a line from three of the water troughs nearest the fire. The pump at each water trough was already manned by someone levering the pump handle as fast as his arms could force it. Down. Up. Down. Up.

Streams of water shooting into the troughs were instantly scooped up by buckets. Each was passed to the next man, who passed it on.

Little of the water went on to Waltman's. Flames spouted upward from three sides of the structure. New fingers of destruction reached constantly skyward, hungrily licking the building for new fuel. The fire was already too hot for anyone to get close enough to throw water on it. What little was attempted erupted in a geyser of steam before it even reached the wood beneath the ravenous flames.

Instead, the brigades threw water on to the buildings on either side of the conflagration, trying with fevered desperation to confine the fire to its original building.

Without consciously doing so, Max looked for Dottie's Millinery & Lace Goods. Relief flooded through him as he remembered Dottie's was on the other side of the street, nearly half a block away.

He stepped into one of the lines where it was stretched farther than the others, and began the rhythmic work of passing full buckets one direction and empty ones the other.

The line curved backward as the heat from Waltman's slammed outward. Three men on the roof of a store next door to Waltman's called for water. Each lowered a rope with a large hook affixed to the end. A fourth line formed, passing water up to the three. They poured it on the roof, where sparks and cinders were already threatening to ignite that building as well.

Realizing they couldn't get to the side of the threatened building any more, a dozen more men scrambled to the roofs of the stores on both sides of Waltman's. Braving the fierce heat, they threw all the water that could be passed to them along the edge of the roof, where it would run down the side walls.

Those walls were already so hot the water evaporated into steam before it reached ground level.

Inside the burning saloon, bottles of whiskey exploded in rhythmic succession. It sounded like a full-blown gun battle, with each shot adding fuel to the already fearsome flames.

'They're never gonna stop it,' Max muttered. 'It's gonna take the whole block.'

Clearly, it could have. By all rights, it should have. Only incredible effort combined with dogged determination kept the flames from spreading.

Those who threw buckets of water on to the edge of the roof whirled back as quickly as their buckets divulged their contents. Even then their eyebrows and the hair in front was singed by the heat with every trip.

As each turned from the edge, he carried, rather

31

than passed, the bucket back to the end of his line, that had formed across the roof. He tossed the empty pail over the side and took a full bucket, passing it along. In that way, each man in the line worked his way steadily forward until it was once again his turn to brave the heat and try to bathe the building's side with water.

Max found himself on the roof, unsure when he abandoned his safe spot in line for its greater need. His turn at the head of the line left him whirling away breathless. His face felt as if it had abruptly blistered and burned. The smell of his own singed hair filled his nostrils.

He stumbled back to the end of the line, dropped his bucket over the side, and accepted a full one from the man at the top of a ladder. Ropes must've been slow, he remembered thinking.

Long before he was ready, he found himself at the head of the line again, racing into the unbearable heat, flinging his bucket of water, and plunging back again where he dared draw a breath.

Trip after trip, each man took his turn. It seemed hours before Waltman's roof collapsed in a geyser of flame. Sparks shot hundreds of feet into the night sky. The side walls fell inward almost immediately.

After the initial surge of heat and flames, that helped. It moved the center of the flames farther from the adjacent buildings. It reduced the ferocity of the heat that the bucket lines had to endure as they sloshed their feeble defense.

They were going to win! Every man engaged in the

battle sensed it almost at the same time. The realization gave new energy, new purpose to their efforts. The speed of the buckets' movements increased noticeably.

By the time they felt safe in stopping the constant wetting of the adjacent buildings' sides, their arms were leaden with exhaustion. Each man stood where he was when the buckets stopped. They stood like sagging statues, each too weary to move out of his place. Each stood with hanging arms and drooping shoulders, sucking in gulps of the night air.

The men on the ladders moved first. Wearily they lowered themselves to the ground, then stood still for several moments to still the trembling of legs that threatened not to hold them up. All moved back from the still flaming pyre that remained of Waltman's Saloon and Gaming Parlor.

Women appeared as if by magic, each holding out drinks to the men who hadn't yet realized the intensity of their thirst. Water, tea, even a little lemonade here and there was guzzled down parched throats so swiftly it was scarcely tasted.

Little by little, the men began to get their breath, to feel alive again, to marvel together at the fruit of their impossible fight.

'By Jing, we done it,' one man with smoke-blackened face muttered.

His words broke a dam of tense and desperate silence. Almost everyone on the street began jabbering to each other. Their torrent of words released the pent-up fear and despair. It was all overwhelmed by the jubilance of hard-fought victory.

Max scanned the crowded street, moving around without joining in on the back-slapping and rehashing of the battle. He hadn't realized he was looking for anyone in particular, until his eyes lit on Dottie. She was handing out cups of water to eager hands that reached for them, as fast as she could fill them.

Max moved to the pump, and began to lever the handle so she could use both hands to fill cups. She glanced at him as he did so. Her eyes lit up when she realized who it was, but she gave no other sign of recognition.

He was surprised at how quickly his arm tired running the pump handle. He was nearer to total exhaustion than he would have believed.

Finally, the incessant line of the thirsty dwindled away. Max found himself staring stupidly at the cup of water held in front of him.

'Your hair's all singed,' Dottie informed him.

He shook his head, willing away the haze that threatened to overwhelm him.

She nudged him with the cup. 'Here. You need to drink this.'

He hadn't been aware that he, too, was thirsty. He hadn't drunk since the fire started. He stared at the cup for another moment, then lifted his arm to take it.

As it spilled across his cracked lips, a rush of thirst welled up from within him. He gulped it down, handing it back in a silent plea for more.

She refilled the cup, but held on to it for a

moment, resisting his grip. 'Don't drink it too fast,' she admonished. 'It'll make you sick.'

He licked his dry, parched lips. He tried to speak, only then realizing his throat was too dry to do so. His first effort resulted only in a croaking sound.

She handed him the cup of cool liquid. 'Here. You better drink another before you try to talk. You sound like a bullfrog.'

He gulped the second cup down as avidly as the first. As he handed it back for yet another refill, he began to gather his senses. He cleared his throat. Even so, his words were husky. 'Didn't know I was that thirsty,' he rasped.

'You were on the roof,' she stated, rather than asked. 'You must have sucked in a lot of smoke and heat.'

He nodded. 'Hotter'n blazes up there.'

She giggled. 'I think it was exactly as hot as blazes up there. Wasn't that what you were fighting?'

A surge of anger inexplicably shot up inside of him, then gave way to the humor of her jibe. 'Is that what that was?' he said. 'I sorta wondered.'

He took a third cup of water from her hand. His hand momentarily closed around hers as he took it. A thrill raced through him at the touch. He frowned.

'What's the matter?' she asked instantly, seeing his sudden frown.

He shook his head, opting to conceal his surprise at his own feelings in the water rather than answer. He drank slower, this time, reveling in the cooling wash of the liquid down his raw throat.

'Throat's gonna be sore tomorrow,' he observed.

'You're going to be sore all over,' she agreed. 'I don't think I've ever seen a group of men work that fast and hard for that long. I didn't think there was a chance they . . . that you could stop it. I was certain the whole block would burn.'

'Me, too,' Max admitted. 'Wonder what started it.'

She snorted, surprising him. 'Yes, I wonder!' She chopped the words off bitterly.

'What do you mean?'

'Oh, this is a great mystery!' Her voice dripped with sarcasm. 'I just can't possibly think of anything that might have started a fire in a business that was taking money out of Virgil McMaster's pocket. It would never, ever occur to him to get rid of any competition.'

Max studied her face in the lessening light of the fire's glow. The lines of her face were etched sharp by its glare. They were even tighter by the clamp of her jaw and the flashing fury in her eyes.

'You think McMaster set it?'

'Of course not. And I'm sure he was where at least twenty people saw him during the time it was being set. But I'd bet my very last nickel that he paid whoever did set it.'

'You think he'd do that?'

She snorted again. 'I know he'd do that. That's the way he always gets what he wants.'

'Meaning what?'

'Meaning just exactly that.'

He studied her in the fading light for a long

moment before he answered. When he did, his still raspy voice was softer. 'Is that what happened to your husband?'

She nodded, looking down abruptly to try to keep him from seeing the tears that welled up. It took her a moment to regain her composure. 'Supposedly he was killed by Indians. It wasn't Indians.'

'How do you know?'

'It couldn't have been. He wouldn't have been there. He didn't die that way.'

'You lost me. I don't know what you're talking about.'

She took a deep breath. 'When Fred didn't come home that night, I started looking. When his horse came home, the neighbors fanned out helping me look. One of them tracked his horse back. He found him clear over by Inyan Kara.'

He frowned. 'What's that?'

She waved a hand southward. 'Over south quite a few miles. It's a mountain the Lakota hold sacred. They don't want white people messing around there, and Fred would never have been there.'

'And someone shot him there?'

'Someone killed him, but not there. He had a Lakota arrow in his back, but it wasn't put there by a bow.'

'Why not?'

'It couldn't have been, at that angle. It was in his back, but it was angled down into his back. If he'd been shot by an Indian, the Indian would have had to have been standing clear above and behind him.

37

Someone stood over him after he was dead and jammed the arrow into him to make it look like Indians killed him.'

'Did you tell anyone that?'

'Lot of good it did,' she replied. 'I also pointed out that his skull was crushed. Someone hit him over the head from behind, hard enough to smash the top of his head in. But there was no blood on the ground where they found him. No blood from the head. No blood from the arrow.'

'Hauled over there and dropped,' Max muttered.

'Of course. Because McMaster had tried to buy our place several times, and Fred wouldn't sell.'

'McMaster did?'

'Well, never personally. It was always someone we didn't know who just happened to look over the place and wanted to buy it.'

'But you think it was McMaster who killed Fred?'

'More likely had one of his "security" men do it.'

They were interrupted by Bud Waltman. His voice sounded tired and old. 'You folks'd just as well go home and try to get some sleep. My crew and I can keep tabs on things to make sure it doesn't do anything but burn itself out. There's nothing more any of you can do. But thank you all for doing all you could.'

Deep silence followed his announcement. Then, by twos and threes, people began to drift away. More than a few stopped by to murmur words of condolence or just to lay an understanding hand on the businessman's shoulder as they left. He acknowledged each, but none took the sag of despondency from his shoulders.

He looks like a dog that got whipped bad, Max thought.

Instead of putting words to the thought, he said, 'May I walk you home?'

Dottie nodded wordlessly. They walked the distance to her house in total silence, both lost in their own world of thoughts.

Awkwardly he spoke at her door. 'I – I'm glad your place was across the street. That was the first thing I thought of.'

'That was sweet of you,' she said. 'Thank you.'

He fumbled in his mind for something to say. He ended with, 'Well, good night.'

'Good night,' she responded. 'Thank you for seeing me home. Again.'

Afraid of what he might say, he merely waved and turned back toward the hotel. It seemed an interminable walk, before he once again propped the chair under the doorknob and collapsed on to the bed.

CHAPTER 5

That the man was dead was obvious. That was as obvious as to how he'd died.

Max sat his horse in the trees, just outside the clearing, studying the scene before him. A man's body swung ever so slightly back and forth, dangling from a rope thrown over a tree limb. Only the wind's moving of the tree caused any motion at all.

The man's hat lay on the ground. Around the clearing, the hoofs of several horses had trampled the grass and churned the ground. Ashes of a small fire sent the barest tendril of smoke upward. A cinch ring, black from having been heated, lay beside two sturdy sticks.

Two steps from the fire, the carcass of a yearling steer was stretched out on its side. It was partially skinned, so the scarring from the brand on the inside of the hide was made visible. Max didn't need to go look at it. He already knew what it would reveal.

'Sure looks like a clear-cut case of brand changing,' he muttered to his horse. 'Sure seems dumb, though. Let's take a closer look, fella.'

He dismounted and walked forward carefully. He pulled a large knife from his belt and sliced the rope, allowing the dead man to drop to the ground. He crumpled as he landed. 'Ain't been dead too long,' Max observed to no one. 'Body ain't stiff yet.'

His own face betraying his revulsion and distaste, he examined that of the dead man. Several large bruises marked it. Dried blood formed a blackened streak from a corner of his mouth to his chin. 'Beat him up some before they hanged him,' he mused.

He stood up straight and released a long, slow breath, studying the inert body at his feet. Then he turned and walked to the carcass of the yearling. It had a bullet hole in the head. If one formed an imaginary X from the eyes to the ears, the hole would have been almost precisely where the lines of the X crossed. 'Good size steer,' he observed. 'Brand change is real clear. Was a triangle. Changed to a Rafter T. Boy, that's crude, though! Nobody buyin' cattle would ever look at that without knowin' it was a worked-over brand. Even a greenhorn would keep the Rafter wider'n the T, and farther up above it.'

He rubbed the back of his neck as he studied the botched brand alteration. 'And if it was Triangle riders that caught him doin' it, why would they kill the steer? It'd be just as obvious if the steer was alive. Anyone in cow country would spot that a mile off. Why did they kill one of their own critters? And if they was going to kill it, why did they leave it lay like that. Hide laid out, inside up, so anyone ridin' by would notice right off that it was an altered brand. Rustler caught red-handed. Hanged on the spot. No questions asked.'

He walked around the clearing, studying the ground, for a long time. 'Three men,' he muttered finally. 'I thought the whole thing was just too pat. It was one of their horses that roped and drug the steer over here. Not the horse that was under that guy when they hanged him.'

He walked back to the silent corpse lying beneath the tree. He cut the rope that bound the man's hands behind him, and removed the noose from around his neck. Max laid his body straight, with the arms at his side. He placed his hat over his face.

He pondered the scene for another long moment. He took another deep breath. Walking back to his horse, he stepped back into the saddle. 'Well, fella, let's see if we can track his horse. If he was a bit hungry, he might graze a while before he heads for home.'

It took him nearly an hour to locate the animal. He had run for a short way, then slowed to a walk, then begun to graze. After a time his grazing had begun to take him in a straight line, almost certainly to wherever he thought of as home.

Returning to the clearing, Max removed the man's bedroll from behind his saddle. He wrapped him tightly in one of his blankets, then hoisted him across the saddle, tying him securely into place.

Taking the reins of the dead man's mount, he resumed his interrupted way.

Three hours later he rode into the yard of the Triangle Ranch.

He wasn't clear into the yard before word of a rider leading a mount bearing a dead man had spread to every corner of the ranch yard. A tall, lean, whip of a man emerged from the house and stepped into the yard to meet him.

'Hate to see a horse carryin' a load like that,' he said. His face was grave. 'I'm Skinny Marshall. Triangle's my place. Whose luck run out?'

Max reined in. 'No idea,' he shook his head. 'Don't know hardly anyone in the country yet. Name's Max Quinn. Found him strung up about eight miles back.'

'Someone hung him?'

'Yup.'

'Know what for?'

'Nope. Not what it was made to look like, though.'

'What d'ya mean? I'm sorry. Git down an' come in. No sense sittin' out here in the sun chinnin'. Max Quinn, ya say?'

Max nodded as he dismounted. 'Glad you're the first one I get to talk to,' he said quickly, noting that ranch hands were beginning to drift across the yard. 'There was a yearling steer skinned out where he was hanged. Had a real crude job of changing a Triangle brand to a Rafter T.'

'What?' Marshall almost shouted. 'Rafter T? That's Fuzz Slocum's brand. Why, Fuzz wouldn't steal a critter if 'is kids was starvin' an' his ranch was gettin' forclosed on!'

'That's what I figured,' Max confirmed. 'The whole thing was way too set up. I can track some. It was one of the guys who hanged him who roped the steer an' drug it to where they hanged 'im.'

Marshall studied his face for a long moment. 'Framed 'im, you're sayin'.'

'I'd bet my eye teeth on it.'

'Now who'd do a thing like that?'

Max shrugged. 'Like I said, I don't know hardly anyone around here yet. Just lookin' for work, and happened to ride on to it.'

Skinny Marshall studied him with some degree of suspicion. 'Why'd you bring 'im here?'

Max met his probing gaze squarely. 'This is where I was headin' anyway, and it seemed the right thing to do. Didn't know where else to take him. Figured you'd know 'im.'

'Why was you headin' here?'

'Met one of your hands in town the other night. Champ Haggler. He told me this was a good outfit to work for.'

The tone of Skinny's gaze softened perceptibly. 'You the one pulled Champ outa the corner he was backed into in town?'

'Yeah, I sorta stepped into that one.'

Skinny grinned abruptly. 'If Champ wasn't stretchin' the truth, ya done a fine job. He's one o' my top hands. I'm obliged.'

'Seemed the thing to do.'

Skinny changed topics abruptly. Turning to one of the approaching cowboys, he raised his voice.

44

Addressing a dried-up, leathery-faced old cowboy, he said, 'Cap, ring the bell and get the hands together.'

Without answering, the old hand turned and walked bow-legged across the yard to the dinner bell, itself an iron triangle hanging near the cook house. He picked up the piece of iron hanging by it, rattling it around the inside of the triangle with enough vigor to shake the dust from sagebrush in a two-mile circle.

By the time Skinny and Max crossed the yard, the crew had gathered. They studied Max and the macabre burden he had in tow with open curiosity. Skinny wasted no time on formalities. 'Any o' you boys catch someone long-ropin' any of our stuff?'

Frowns and shaken heads met his query. When nobody offered any response, he continued, addressing Cap this time. 'Anyone been sent over ta Dugan's Valley for anything?'

Cap shook his head. 'We got some steers over there, but I ain't sent nobody ta check on 'em in a couple weeks.'

Skinny changed tack. 'Anyone know who'd be wantin' ta get rid o' Fuzz Slocum?'

Idle curiosity and confusion was instantly replaced with obvious concern, but nobody answered for a long time. Finally a cowboy said, 'Somethin' happen to Fuzz?'

'I'm bettin' that's him,' Skinny confirmed, waving toward the body draped across the saddle.

'What happened to 'im?' another queried.

'Someone hung 'im.'

Jaws dropped. Men looked at one another, then at

Max, then back to Skinny.

'Someone hanged 'im,' Skinny continued, 'and went to a whole lot o' trouble to make it look like he was caught red-handed changin' the brand on one o' my steers.'

Anger and disbelief gave a sharp edge to the cowpoke who responded. 'That's bull! Fuzz wouldn't eat a pickle outa the barrel at the store without payin' for it.'

A murmur of agreement indicated that every hand on the place was in total agreement. 'Well, it ain't the first underhanded deal happenin' around this country,' Skinny observed. 'Ain't likely to be the last. We'll figger it out sooner or later.'

He turned to his foreman. 'Cap, sorry to dump this on ya. You an' one of the boys check 'im out. Make sure it's Fuzz. Then we'll take 'im home.'

'You comin' with us?'

Skinny nodded. 'Me an' the missus will both go. Hattie'll be needin' a woman to talk to. Tuffy, you ride over to Matson's place. Tell 'em what happened. Make sure they know it was a put-up deal, that we don't think for a minute Fuzz was stealin' our stock. Fuzz an' Hattie was real close to Jim an' Katie. Hattie'll be wantin' 'em there.'

He turned back to Max. 'You say you're lookin' for a job.'

Max nodded silently.

'I owe ya that,' Skinny declared. 'For bringin' Fuzz in here, as well as for bein' there when Champ needed someone to hold his hand.'

An instant change in the decorum of the group met his words. All eyes whipped teasingly to Champ Haggler. He turned noticeably red.

The moment of levity disappeared as swiftly as it had come. Glancing at the corpse on the horse turned every look dour again.

Skinny addressed Max. 'You can put your horse up in the barn. Hay an' grain's there. Find an empty bunk in the bunkhouse. We pay same's most places. Thirty a month an' found. Five horses besides your own for your string. You pick 'em from the remuda. Ammunition's furnished. Spendin' money as ya need it. Whatever ya got comin' when ya leave. We've already ate supper, but Ling'll rustle you up a bait o' grub if you stop at the cook house when you're done puttin' up your horse.'

Max nodded silently. Champ stepped forward. 'C'mon. I'll show ya where stuff is.'

CHAPTER 6

Two lamps cast flickering shadows around the bunkhouse. Tired hands talked as they prepared to roll into their bunks. The mood had been somber. Talk had all been of the recent troubles plaguing the area. Now the death of a well-known, highly respected small rancher deepened the troubles greatly.

Three of the hands, obvious gunfighters, seemed least disturbed. They had been brought on to the crew in direct response to the growing crisis. While they showed the least emotion, they paid a great deal of attention to the cleaning and oiling of their weapons. They were clearly gearing themselves for trouble.

When talk waned, one of the hands sought to lighten the mood.

'I heard the trout was bitin' along Beaver Crick.'

Another took up the subject immediately, as though eager for the change of topics. 'That's a fact. I had some time on my hands yesterday. Threw a hook and line with a worm on it into that big old pool where them five boulders are. It hadn't any more'n hit the water when a trout hit it. Big ol' thing. Pertneart more'n I could do to eat 'im.'

'You ate 'im? Without even bringin' him home to share?'

'Dang right. Made me a little fire and cooked him right there.'

'Why didn't ya bring 'im home?'

'What, one trout? Split among all you guys?'

'You coulda caught more, if they was bitin' that good.'

'Sure! An' come home an' tell Cap I didn't have enough work to do, so I spent the afternoon fishin'! Do you know what Cap'd do?'

Several chuckled. One young cowboy, with a rueful tone of voice, said, 'I sure do. He'd put ya to cleanin' out stalls in the barn for the next three days.'

That brought more laughter.

Half-a-dozen stories followed, of catching trout and failing to get a bite when others were having great luck.

Milt Winslow spoke up for the first time. 'All that puts me in mind o' that stretch o' Hickory Crick above the big canyon. Now there's a spot to fish!'

One of the cowboys responded instantly. 'I've only been over there twice. I ain't goin' back, unless I gotta.'

'Why not?' a voice enquired.

'Too many rattlesnakes,' the first cowboy responded.

'I ain't never been no place where I seen so many rattlers so close together.'

'Skeert o' snakes, youngster?'

He shook his head emphatically. 'I ain't scared of 'em, but I sure don't like 'em. The last time I was over there, I killed seven of 'em, one afternoon. When they're that thick, there's just too much chance o' gettin' bit.'

Winslow recovered the lead in the conversation. 'It's snaky over there, all right. 'Bout the snakiest place I ever seen. But the fishin's worth it.'

That got the response he wanted. The youngster asked immediately, 'What's the most fish you ever caught over there, Milt?'

Milt picked up a tin can and spit tobacco juice into it, and set it back down on the floor. He waited for several seconds, to be sure everyone in the bunkhouse was listening. One of the old hands nudged another in the ribs and winked knowingly at him.

'It ain't so much the number of fish,' Milt said, 'it's more the size. Why I was over there one time when I had pertneart the whole day to kill. Took me an extra line and several hooks. I fished eight or ten big pools along that crick, and I couldn't get me so much as a nibble.'

'That's the way it is when I fish,' a faceless voice agreed.

Milt nodded and spit again. As he set the can back on the floor he said, 'Well, I tried worms. I tried grasshoppers. I tried three or four different kind o' bugs. I tried lettin' 'em drift on top o' the water. I tried tyin' a rock to the line and makin' it sink to the bottom. They jist wasn't bitin'.'

Silence gripped the room, waiting for what was to come. 'That there's when I hit on the idea. I decided what I needed was a little frog. Trout'll jist go plumb nuts over a frog.'

'There's some over there all right,' someone observed.

'They is for a fact,' Milt agreed. 'But hard ta find in daylight, they is. But I started along the edge o' the crick, a-lookin' anyhow. That's when I seen 'im.'

By now, every hand was sitting on the edge of a bunk, leaning forward. 'Seen what?' somebody asked.

'Well, sir,' Milt replied, 'there was one o' the biggest rattlesnakes I ever seen, all stretched out there. Better'n three feet long, he was. Big around as my arm. Rattlin' ta beat the band. An' he had a frog, oh, maybe half swallered.'

The crew nearly held their breath, waiting for him to continue. He spit again before he did.

'Well, thet there frog was still wigglin'. Ya know how a snake swallers somethin'. They sorta take their jaw outa joint or somethin', and then work it down real slow. They can't spit it out. They can't swaller any faster. They're just stuck there.'

'So, did you kill it?'

Milt took his time spitting and setting his can down again. Then he shook his head. 'Naw, I guess I'm gettin' kinda soft in my old age. Jist didn't seem right somehow, ta whack his head off, while he's all helpless like that there, an' all.'

'So what did you do?' someone demanded.

Milt took his time. 'Well, I had ta figger me out a way ta make 'im spit that frog out, while he was still alive some. Trout, they won't bite on a dead frog. If he wiggles jist a little, they'll go after 'im like crazy. But not if he's dead. Then I got me an idea.'

He waited several seconds. 'I always got my pocket flask along, ya know. Jist in case I get snake-bit. Good idea to always have a few swallers o' whiskey along. So I takes out my pocket flask an' pulls the cork out. Then I put my foot on top o' that rattler. I reached down and grabbed the front of is nose, an' pried his mouth open.'

'You pried his mouth open with your hand?' an incredulous voice echoed.

'I pried his mouth open,' Milt repeated. 'Of course, pryin' up that hard on 'is mouth tipped 'is head straight up, so it was easier'n anything to pour som o' that whiskey down his throat.'

'He swallowed it?'

'He didn't have no choice. Swaller it or choke. But I'm tellin' ya, I ain't never seen a rattler go nuts like that afore. He started a-twistin' an' floppin' around so hard he was two feet off the ground part o' the time. He acted like he was havin' a full-fledged conniption fit. He flopped around like that for three or four minutes, than he spit that frog out so hard it flew a good yard, and he slithered off into the brush.'

Open mouths and slack jaws sought to digest the

strangeness of the story. Milt took full advantage, spitting again before continuing.

'I run over there and grabbed the frog, and danged if he wasn't still wigglin' some. He was bigger'n I'd thought, though. I wasn't sure a trout'd even go for 'im. But after all that, I sure wasn't gonna not try. So I stuck 'im on my biggest hook, an' tossed it out into a big pool.'

'What happened?' a breathless cowboy asked.

'Well, sir, it hadn't no sooner hit the water when somethin' hit that thing like a freight train. It danged near jerked me plumb into the crick. I hauled away on that string for all I was worth, for, oh, I bet pert-neart twenty minutes, afore I hauled in the biggest German Brown trout I ever seen in my whole life. I bet that thing was two and a half feet long.'

'You got him landed?'

'Betcher boots I got 'im landed,' Milt bragged.

He waited long enough to spit again, then continued. 'I had that hook set plumb hard, too. Took me a while to get it pried loose, and him a floppin' and fightin' the whole time. I jist got the hook out, and I felt somethin' against the back o' my leg. I looked down, and you'll never in a million years guess what I seen.'

Half a minute of silence finally elicited an eager, 'What was it, Milt?'

'It was that same dang rattlesnake,' Milt replied.

He waited just an instant, then added, 'He'd brung me another frog.'

Silence hung suspended in every corner of the

room, before it was shattered by raucous laughter from a dozen throats at once.

Holding his sides with laughter, the old cowpoke who had nudged his buddy at the beginning of the story pointed at the youngster. 'Did you see Bobby's face? He was soakin' up every word o' that yarn like a sponge.'

'That ain't fair!' Bobby protested. 'I was believing you!'

Another chorus of laughter erupted at his expense. He swore and rolled into his bunk, pulling up a blanket and turning his back on the room.

'Boy, you sure had me goin'!' another young cowboy admitted. 'I was swallowin' every word of it too.'

His sheepish confession elicited another. 'Yeah, me too. Good story, Milt.'

Cowboys quickly learn to grab what sleep they can when they can. In fifteen minutes the lamps had been blown out, and every man in the room was sound asleep.

Except Max. He continued to turn the events of the past week over and over in his mind. A knot in his stomach assured him there was worse to come.

CHAPTER 7

His instincts told him he was being watched. Try as he might, he could neither see nor hear a reason for the feeling. Nonetheless, his skin continued to crawl from time to time.

He rode down along a long hogback, then angled downward. A finger of timber marked the end of a heavier stand. Beyond it was tall grass and brush that indicated water. It would be a good spot for strays to wander.

Then he saw the horse. Mane and tail streaming, it was running hard. Its saddle was empty.

Max frowned thoughtfully. 'Somebody got dumped,' he muttered. 'Or shot.'

He pondered catching the horse, or backtracking it. He decided it would be most prudent to try to find its rider first.

He rode quickly to the first point he had spotted the galloping animal. Its trail was easy to pick up in the tall grass. He followed it at a brisk trot, slowing when he entered scattered timber. Watching all around carefully, he followed across shallow draws, and finally up the flat bottom of a heavily timbered, narrow valley.

He had ridden for three-quarters of an hour before he saw her. He jerked his horse to a standstill and stared in disbelief.

One of the most beautiful women he had ever seen stared back at him across a small clearing. Long black hair streamed down from a perfectly formed, olive-skinned face. The white blouse pulled tight in front, accentuated an alluring figure. Her long riding skirt was brightly embroidered in brilliant colors. Only her boots showed wear. They indictaed a custom of a great deal of riding. The rowels on her spurs were surprisingly large for a woman.

All this he took in at a glance. Then she flashed a dazzling smile.

Momentarily speechless, he took off his hat and smiled back. The thought crossed his mind suddenly that he was glad he had bathed the night before.

'Did you see my horse?' she asked.

He nodded, working to clear his throat silently. 'I saw him running. I decided to backtrack him before I tried to catch him. I thought someone might be in trouble.'

Her smile flashed again. 'I am afraid I am exactly that,' she admitted. 'But it might have been worse.'

'How's that?'

'I might have fallen off when my horse was first scared by the mountain lion. He ran away with me.'

Who wouldn't want to run away with you? Max

56

thought silently.

Unaware of his thoughts, she continued uninterrupted. 'I managed to stay on him until he had outrun the lion. Then I didn't dodge quickly enough. A tree branch knocked me out of the saddle. My poor horse is still out there somewhere, running for his life, and I'm standing here in the timber hoping the lion isn't still hungry.'

'Then I'm glad I decided to backtrack first,' Max declared. 'I wouldn't want anyone as beautiful as you getting eaten by a cougar.'

Her smile brightened the sunlight by several degrees. 'Why thank you! How very gallant of you to say that. My name is Carlita Daniels.'

'Max Quinn,' Max responded.

'Will you be my knight in shining armor and help me find my horse, Max Quinn'

'I can't think of anything I'd rather do,' he said, meaning it from the depth of his being.

He rode over beside her and removed his foot from the left stirrup, just beside her. She lifted her foot into the stirrup and swung up easily behind him. The thought ran unbidden through his mind that it was a shame the saddle's cantle was between them.

It mattered little. She slid her arms around his stomach and pressed against his back. He was suddenly aware of nothing in the world except the feel of her breasts pressing against him, her arms around him, her hands never quite still against his stomach and chest.

Trying to hide his discomfiture, he replaced his

hat and lifted the reins, nudging his horse into motion. He knew instinctively she was too skilled a horsewoman to need to hold on to him. He also knew he wasn't about to point that out to her.

'Pretty isolated place for a lady to be riding,' he observed, when they had ridden a short ways.

'I ride here a lot,' she retorted. 'I like it here. So do our cattle. I try to keep track of them.'

'You have a place close to here?'

'The Double D. Have you seen our brand?'

He waved his hand southward. 'I saw a couple dozen cows and calves about two miles south.'

'Good,' she responded. 'That's where I hazed them the other day. There's better grass and water there.'

'You and your husband have the place over south there?'

She giggled unexpectedly. 'I do not have a husband,' she informed him. 'My father owns the Double D. It is not that big for a ranch. My mother was from Sonora. She was very beautiful, but she has died, so it is only just me and my father. We are only big enough to hire one hand. That is why I have to help keep track of our cattle. Besides, I like to do it.'

Max was at a loss to explain why her announcement sent such a thrill through him. He ignored it, chatting with her about the weather, their year's calf crop, whatever small talk he could think of.

'Where are you from?' she asked eventually. 'I don't remember seeing you before.'

'Haven't been in the country long,' he admitted.

'Got tired of working out on the flats. Thought I'd find a job with a place closer to the mountains.'

'The Black Hills are not the very big mountains,' she observed.

'Bigger than anything out on the flats,' he countered. 'It's nice country.'

'And have you found a job?'

'Yeah, I did. I hired on with the Triangle the other day.'

The abrupt and flat way she said 'Oh' rattled him. So did the sudden way she moved slightly away from him. He felt as if there were suddenly a mile of space between them, even though her arms were still around him.

'Is there something wrong with that?'

'I am disappointed. I thought I was a better judge of character than that.'

'What's wrong with working for the Triangle?'

'It is one of the big ranches,' she accused. 'They are all working together.'

'Working together to do what?'

'To get rid of the rest of us. To get rid of all the small ranchers.'

'What makes you say that?' he demanded.

'It is the fact. That is all. I think that you are a gunfighter, like the others they are hiring. Is that why you have really come here, Max Quinn?'

'I'm not a gunfighter,' he argued. 'I just hired on as a cowhand.'

'There are some who work for him who are just gunfighters.'

He couldn't think of an answer that would contradict her flat statement. He knew three of the hands in the bunkhouse were only there for their skill with guns.

He tried to divert the conversation slightly. 'How are they trying to get rid of the little guys?'

He felt her shrug. It seemed as if she might have moved ever so slightly back toward him. 'They buy out the ones that will sell; they try to scare the ones they can scare. They find ways. They took away the deed to Margaret and Richard Blanchard's ranch. They took it in a poker game. I am sure they cheated.'

'One of the big ranchers did that?'

He felt her shrug again. 'He would not tell me who it was. He only said that he lost it fair and square in a poker game. Margaret will die from a broken heart, I think, wherever they have gone.'

'Who moved on to their place?'

The shrug again. 'Nobody, yet. That is why I am sure it was one of the big ranches. Probably the Triangle. I know he is an evil man.'

'Skinny?'

'*Sí*. Yes. I'm sorry. Being so close with you makes me not think so straight. With my mother I spoke always in Spanish. Sometimes I forget and do that. Yes, Preston Marshall is an evil man.'

'Why do you say that?'

'Because I know. He has tried so many times to make my father sell to him. Then he tried to make me get my father to sell, but I will not do it.'

'He tried to get you to persuade your father?'

'*Sí*. I mean, yes.'

'Why would you do that?'

'Because of his threats. He is an evil man.'

'He threatened you?'

'He did not say exactly anything that I could say was a threat. But I know what he meant. He said it two times.'

'Said what?'

'He said that it was not a good country for a young lady like me, because I ride alone too much. He knows I have to do that, because my father cannot afford more cowboys. But a young woman riding alone so much is likely to have to pay a price that no woman should ever have to pay. That is what he says to me. Two times. So I must persuade my father to sell to him so that will not happen. It is not a threat, but it was very much a threat. Two times it was very much a threat.'

They rode in silence a long way. Knowing before he said it that it would sound lame, he finally said, 'I'm sorry. I didn't have Skinny pegged for that kind.'

It was an adequate response, even if it sounded lame to him. The distance between them was gone again. His spirits soared, in spite of the questions that niggled at the corners of his mind. 'There's your horse,' he announced.

A quarter-mile ahead a big black gelding raised his head from munching the grass. Max's horse whinnied a greeting the gelding answered.

'Will I need to dab a rope on him?' Max asked.

'Oh, no. He is very well trained. Now that he is not afraid of the lion, I can walk up to him any place.'

He nodded in silence. When he drew rein beside the animal he slipped his foot out of the left stirrup. Holding him more tightly than necessary, she put her foot in the stirrup and swung to the ground. She stayed there beside him, her hand on his leg, looking up at him.

'Thank you for rescuing me from a very long walk,' she said. Her eyes melted everything inside of him. 'You said you have seen our ranch?'

He nodded, and was rewarded with that incomparable smile again. 'Good. Then you will stop by whenever you are anywhere near? I would so very much like to get to know you better, Max.'

'Well now, with an invitation like that, you might have to hire a whole posse to get rid of me.'

She giggled merrily. She said, 'I surely hope so,' and turned away. She caught up the reins of her horse, stepped lightly into the saddle, and rode away.

As she did, she turned in the saddle and blew him a kiss.

He didn't know why he felt as if it would blow him out of the saddle. He just knew he would certainly make it a point to see more of Carlita Daniels.

CHAPTER 8

Questions boiled in Max's mind. Intermingled with them, visions of Carlita kept sending his mind wandering in directions that had nothing to do with who he worked for. They certainly had nothing to do with Triangle strays he hadn't seen any of anyway.

'Wonder why Cap sent me clear over here lookin' for strays,' he asked his horse. 'And I wonder if Carlita is the one who was watchin' me? Nah. She couldn't have even known I was in the country. Or cared.'

In answer, the horse merely waggled his ears.

'Sundance can't be more'n an hour's ride that-away,' he mused.

As if in answer, the horse turned his head and glanced that direction.

'Let's take a look-see around town,' Max decided. 'It'll still be early when we get there. It shouldn't make a whole lot of difference to Marshall whether I sleep in the hotel or out on the ground somewhere. 'Specially if he doesn't know.'

He put his horse up in the livery stable and rented

the same room at the hotel. Then he walked down the street. The ashes of Waltman's saloon and gambling hall still smelled of smoke and treachery. He made a mental note to nose around the back side of the destroyed building later.

McMaster's Good Times was certainly reaping the benefit of Waltman's fire. The loss of his biggest competitor had visibly increased business. There wasn't an empty chair in the saloon, and very few empty spaces at the bar.

Almost at once his attention was drawn to a crowd of people surrounding one of the tables. He strolled over, edging his way through until he could see. A poker game was in progress. By the size of the stacks of chips, it was high stakes indeed.

One of the players bet heavily on three jacks. The other players had folded, leaving only him and the dealer.

'Who's the cowboy?' Max asked a young man standing beside him.

'Phil Henry,' the young man responded at once. 'Sold a bunch of his calves. Be lucky if he gets home with a nickel of it.'

'Losing some, huh?'

'Been losin' steady. Dangest thing I ever seen. You watch. The dealer'll have a hand that'll just barely beat 'im.'

Max eased back to the back of the crowd. He worked his way forward again, until he was standing at the front of the crowd, just at the right side of the dealer. As if to mark the young cowpoke as a seer, the dealer laid down a straight and raked in the pot.

The rancher swore. 'It don't make no difference what I have, you always have one up on me,' he complained. 'That kinds luck can't last.'

Max's eyebrows knit into furrows that met at the bridge of his nose. He didn't even wait to see what the guy had before he reached for the pot, he thought.

He watched closely for three more hands. In one of them, another player won a small pot. The second hand the rancher won, but again, only a small amount of chips. The dealer had held three sixes, but hadn't raised the bets. The rancher held three nines.

The third hand the rancher bet more heavily. Again everybody dropped out except him and the dealer. The dealer called and raised.

Phil studied his cards again furtively. He counted the chips in front of him. He announced the total. 'I'm raisin' ya with everythin' I got.'

The crowd gasped. The dealer thought it over for a brief moment.

'I'll call you, and raise you another three thousand dollars.'

The crowd gasped again. Phil swallowed hard. 'I ain't got another three thousand.'

'You folding then?'

Phil looked at the huge stack of chips in the center of the table. He swallowed again. He wiped his hands across his face. 'I'll call you,' he announced. 'I'm good for it.'

The dealer smiled faintly. 'What do you have for security?'

'You got my word. That's as good as gold.'

'I'm sure it is,' the dealer soothed. 'I'm sure not challenging that. But the boss won't let me take any bets above the chips on the table unless there's something for security. It's not my choice. I'd take your word in a minute.'

Phil thought it over for several seconds. 'What d'ya want?'

The dealer shrugged. 'What do you have worth three thousand dollars?'

'My cattle. My place.'

The dealer nodded. 'Either one. The place'd be fine. Just write out a deed for it, and I can take that for the three thousand.'

Phil turned beet red. He sneaked another peek at his cards. He swallowed hard. 'Gimme a piece o' paper an' a pencil,' he said.

Almost as if by magic, a sheet of paper and a pencil appeared. He scribbled hurriedly on it and tossed it into the pot. 'You're called,' he announced.

'Fair enough,' the dealer agreed. 'How many?'

'Two,' the rancher called for, tossing two cards into the center of the table. The dealer flipped two cards across the table.

The dealer also tossed two of his own cards into the center of the table.

'Dealer takes two,' he said, dealing himself the first card. His deal of the second card was arrested abruptly. Max's hand shot forward, grasping the dealer's hand and the deck of cards in an iron grip.

A gasp went up from the crowd around the table.

Jerking and pulling his best, the dealer was unable to move. The card he was in the act of dealing was clearly coming from the bottom of the deck. He tried to drop the card that was halfway out from the bottom of the deck, but the steely grip of Max's hand wouldn't allow even that much movement. It was as if he were frozen in time, caught in the act.

The dealer looked around frantically, surrounded by a suddenly hostile crowd.

'I think it's somewhat against the rules to deal off the bottom of the deck, ain't it?' Max's voice was soft and low, but pregnant with danger.

'You was cheatin' me!' Phil Henry exclaimed. 'You been cheatin' me the whole time!'

'That's what I'd call it,' Max agreed. 'He's dealt seconds, dealt off the bottom, and marked every card in the deck.'

He waited several seconds to give his words time to soak in with everyone in the crowd. Then he said, 'I think that means you own all the chips in that pot, and all of them that are left in front of the dealer too.'

It took only an instant for the rancher to take advantage of the opportunity. Whipping off his hat, he swept his chips and the dealer's into it. 'Anyone else think you got a claim on any of it?' he asked around the table.

Eyes darted from him to Max to the dealer and back to the rancher, but nobody spoke up. 'Then I'll just go cash in my chips an' go home,' Phil announced.

Max released the dealer's hand and stepped back.

In a move too swift for the eye to follow, the dealer stood and extended his hand. A two-shot derringer had somehow materialized in his hand.

Two shots roared as one. Activity in the saloon and gambling hall came to an instant halt. People looked around fearfully, trying to determine if they were in danger. Several dived under the closest table.

The dealer stood glaring at Max for a full second. The angry glare in his eyes turned blank. Then he took a step backward. A red stain spread rapidly across his vest. A tendril of smoke wafted up from the barrel of his derringer. The gun slipped from his fingers and clattered to the floor. He followed it an instant later.

Max holstered his .45. He watched the dealer, ignoring the sudden buzz of voices. There was no movement from the inert gambler.

Phil Henry was the first to speak. 'I don't know who you are, mister. I sure don't know how you unlimbered that hogleg o' yours that fast. But I'm much obliged. He'd'a stole my place from me if you hadn't been here.'

A coarse voice bellowed, 'What's going on here?'

The crowd parted, or were shoved aside. A tall, broad-shouldered man in a very expensive broadcloth suit pushed himself to the front. He stopped when he saw the dealer on the floor. His eyes darted around the circle of faces. 'Who in blazes shot my dealer?'

'I did,' Max replied. His voice was soft, but his words were hard as flint.

Before the newcomer could respond, another

voice piped up. 'Your dealer was cheatin', Virg. This here guy caught 'im red-handed. Grabbed his hand and the deck o' cards both. Held on so's everyone could see. He was dealin' himself a card straight from the bottom o' the deck.'

A murmur of agreement rippled through the crowd.

Virgil McMaster's eyes darted around the crowd, to the dead dealer, then back to Max. His voice was taut with ill-controlled anger. 'I don't know who you are, mister, but this is the second time you've been a problem in my place. From now on, if you have a problem with any of my dealers, you come to me. I won't stand for anyone taking the law into his own hands with my people.'

The softness left Max's voice. 'You protect card cheats?' he asked.

The implication that the dealer was cheating by his orders was unmistakable, but unspoken. McMaster turned a deep shade of red. His eyes bored holes through Max. 'I told you how to deal with it, if you think one of my dealers is cheating,' he gritted.

'Is that to be before he shoots me with his hideout gun, or after?'

The red of McMaster's face deepened to purple. He opened his mouth twice to respond, then closed it again. Three large men had appeared behind him. Max could feel the presence of at least one, probably more, behind him. Even so, he didn't think the owner would dare risk doing anything in defense of his dealer, who had been so clearly demonstrated to be cheating. It was a spot he was obviously not used

69

to being in.

'Just get out!' he grated finally. 'And if you interfere with one of my dealers again, you won't live to tell about it.'

'Then you best make sure you have honest dealers,' Max responded.

He and McMaster glared at each other. It was McMaster who broke off the wordless confrontation of stares first. He whirled on his heel and stomped away.

'Get that piano player on the job,' he ordered, as he stalked away. 'And get somebody up there on that stage singing. This is a gaming hall, not a mortuary.'

People scurried to obey and restore a festive air to the place. Two of the burly men who had appeared with McMaster picked up the body of the dealer and carried him away. An old man appeared with a bucket of sawdust and spread it quickly over the blood on the floor.

The crowd around Max began to thin. He took advantage of the fact and eased his way toward the door. Before he stepped outside, he looked carefully around. If anyone had been ordered to follow him, he couldn't pick him out.

He went out the door and stepped swiftly sideways, flattening himself against the front of the building. He looked up and down the street. Nothing seemed awry.

Seems odd, he mused. It looks like at least a town marshal would show up when there's shooting goin' on.

He chalked up another point to McMaster's control of the town. Still watching around warily, he made his way back to the hotel.

CHAPTER 9

Max slept fitfully. He was surrounded by gamblers with derringers in their hands. He whipped out his gun and fired as fast as he could, but nothing resulted. The threatening derringers continued their mindless, over-under stare of death. He braced himself for the impact of the bullets that failed to come.

Then he was abruptly in some remote corner of the range he could not identify, surrounded by riflemen. His dead horse lay on his leg, pinning him helplessly to the ground. He fought frantically to stretch to the rifle in his saddle scabbard, but couldn't quite reach it. He jerked and twisted against the restraining grip on his leg, to no avail.

A noise down the hotel hallway roused him just enough for the dream to break into fragments and melt away. Moonlight bathed the room in soft light. He glanced at the chair propped under the door knob. He muttered against the disturbing dreams and went back to sleep.

She came again to him then, sometime between the half-waking check of his door and morning. Her incredible beauty, more than her abrupt presence in his hotel room, made his heart stop. It didn't occur to him to wonder how the wind blew her silken hair so softly inside a closed room. He merely watched, mesmerized.

His eyes traveled from her shining hair to the deep brown, almost black, of her eyes. They reached out to him, glistening with ineffable love and longing. Her lips were slightly parted, half smiling, entirely inviting.

His eyes drifted down her flawless form. He noted again the lift of her breasts within the spotless white of her flowing gown. He followed the contours of her body, as the gown gently moved to accent each flawless feature. He studied her enticing form clear to the dainty ankles and bare feet, then slowly back up to the perfect face.

Loneliness and desire welled up within him. He wanted her more than he could remember wanting anything in his life. He remembered the icy pangs that had shot through him when he touched her, in that other dream. He felt again the panic that had risen in him at his inability to rinse her grip from his arm.

Mingled together, fear and desire rose like a wildfire, sweeping everything else aside in a mindless determination to have her, to possess her, to love her.

She lifted her arms, extending them to him in open invitation. Her smile radiated pure love and open desire to satisfy his every need.

He shook his head in his sleep, reaching out for her even as he fought against his desires. Her smile broadened, showing twin rows of perfect teeth. For just an instant the tip of her tongue appeared between them, then disappeared again.

He felt himself rising from the bed, as if propelled by some force other than his own will. Even as his head continued to shake a frantic refusal, his arms lifted toward the vision of beauty that beckoned him. He felt her hunger for him as if it were an extension of the ache of his own heart.

As she neared him, however, he again backed away, instead of enfolding her in his arms as he longed to do.

She appeared not to notice. She continued to approach, reaching, offering more than ample compensation for all the lonely nights. He knew suddenly he couldn't stand to spend another night alone. He couldn't think of anything except clasping her to himself and never separating from her again. All reason was swept away. All reticence was gone. He willed her into his arms.

Even as he did, something deep within him propelled him backward, away from her. His shoulders struck the wall of the hotel room. She was right before him. She reached out to enfold him to herself.

While everything he could sense within himself responded eagerly, hungrily for all that she offered, he twisted away. He hit the floor with a jar that completely awakened him. His feet were tangled in the blanket. He cast desperately around the room, searching for the vision of desire and beauty. The room was empty.

He slid backward on the floor until his back was against the wall and slowly untangled the blanket from around his ankles. Emptiness gaped within him, as if some great portion of his being had been scooped away, leaving only empty shell. Greater loneliness than he could ever remember swept through him. For the first time in years, a tear ran down his cheek.

He shook his head angrily. 'Stupid dream again,' he complained.

He stood and paced the small room for several minutes. He stood at the window, staring out at the silence of the sleeping town.

He turned back to the bed, wishing it were daylight so he could forget about sleep. He didn't know how long it was before sleep finally returned, but when he next awakened, he had his wish. Sunlight streamed into the small room. Dust moved slowly in the brightness of the beams that shone through the window.

He muttered words of self-remonstrance at oversleeping. Splashing water into the basin on the stand, he washed, then shaved quickly. Looking below to ensure there was nobody walking there, he flung the soapy water out.

He dressed, checked the loads in his .45, then removed the chair propped beneath the door knob.

Breakfast, and three cups of strong, scalding coffee at the café in the hotel brightened his mood perceptibly.

Leaving the hotel he walked down the main street of Sundance. He watched around carefully, but saw no indication that anyone made note of his presence.

As if of their own volition, his feet carried him to the burned ruins of Waltman's Saloon and Gaming Parlor. He walked carefully around burned and jagged timbers.

At what had been the rear of the establishment, he began searching in earnest. Moving aside debris and wreckage that had tumbled down from the second floor, he exposed a short portion of the base of the burned wall.

Several people on the sidewalks stopped to watch him for a moment, then moved on. He looked around self-consciously, then shrugged his shoulders. He stretched out on the ground, supporting himself by hands and toes to avoid being coated with the black ashes. Thrusting his nose against the ground where it met the base of the wall, he sniffed carefully.

He pulled his feet back under him and stood. He nodded once.

He walked to a water trough by a hitch rail and washed the ashes and soot from his hands. He shook the water from them, and let the light Wyoming air dry them.

Then he stopped at the marshal's office.

'You the town marshal?' he asked the puffy-faced

man behind a scarred desk.

'That'd be me.' His watery eyes studied Max carefully. 'Who're you?'

'Name's Max Quinn.'

'Ralph Small,' the marshal responded. 'You killed Smooth Louie.'

'Who?'

'Louie. One o' Virg's dealers.'

'He was smooth,' Max agreed. 'Crookeder than a dog's hind leg, though.'

'So I heard. What're you here for?'

'Just wanted to make sure you weren't looking for me.'

'For what?'

'For killing the dealer.'

The marshal shrugged. 'Whole lot of people saw it. They all said it was a clear case of self-defense. I got no call to fault ya for that.'

Max nodded. 'I was some surprised you didn't come a-runnin' when you heard the shots.'

The marshal shrugged again. 'Virg pretty well takes care o' what happens inside his place. If he needs anythin' from me, he'll send someone to fetch me.'

Max pondered the statement for a while. 'Been marshal long?'

'Pertnear a year.'

'Much of a problem keeping a lid on things?'

The marshal's watery eyes turned cautious. 'Why would that interest you?'

It was Max's turn to shrug. 'Just wondered. That's

all. The big ranchers appear to be afraid the little guys are out to get them. The little guys think the same of the big ranchers. Then there's all the prospectors and gold fever spilling over from the Black Hills. Seems like it could be a pretty volatile situation.'

'A pretty what?'

'Volatile . . . it seems like the lid could blow off of this country most any time.' The marshal gave his characteristic shrug again. 'As long as it stays outa town, it ain't no skin off my nose.'

'And if it doesn't, I 'spect Virg'll pretty well take care of it.'

The marshal nodded. 'Mind you, I'm capable of stepping in if I need to, so don't go gettin' no bright ideas about tryin' to pull anything.'

Max held his hands up just below shoulder level, palms outward. 'I'm not looking for any trouble.'

The marshal nodded in clear dismissal. 'Keep it that way.'

He returned his attention to the papers he was fumbling through on his desk. He didn't even acknowledge Max's departure.

'Sorry excuse for a lawman,' Max muttered, as he walked away.

CHAPTER 10

Max wasn't sure when or why he decided to walk to Dottie's store. He simply found himself walking in the front door. He was suddenly terrified the place would be filled with women, and he would be the only man there.

Relief swept through him when he saw the store was empty of customers. Dottie looked up from behind the long counter. Her eyes lit up instantly. A smile spread across her face. 'Why, Max! How good to see you. Are you shopping for a corset, by chance?'

His grin answered hers. 'Now how did you know that?'

'And just why would you want one of those?'

'Well, I figured if I bought one for myself, I could study the thing and figure out how to get one unfastened when I want to.'

He was rewarded by the sudden flush that colored her face. She opened her mouth twice to speak, then closed it again. Her eyes danced. 'OK,' she said eventually, 'I guess I asked for that one. You're one up on me.'

'That's no small accomplishment,' He congratulated himself. 'You're pretty quick on the trigger.'

'What brings you here?' she said, changing the subject.

'Hunger. Hunger and loneliness. I thought I'd see if a beautiful woman would consider accompanying me to dinner at the hotel dining-room. That would solve both of my terrible maladies. At least for the moment.'

'Well, if I happen to see a beautiful woman walk by, I could ask her for you.'

Sweeping off his hat in mock chivalry, he spoke in an exaggerated Southem drawl. 'Why, ma'am, there just couldn't be a woman any more beautiful than you are. Why, you're prettier than a rose growing up in the middle of a hog pen.'

She laughed out loud. 'Now that's the strangest compliment I have ever been paid. It was a compliment, wasn't it? You're not insinuating my store is a hog pen, are you?'

Surprised by the question, he stammered, 'No! No, that's not what I meant at all. All I meant was . . . OK. We're quits. You could have waited an hour or two before getting even.'

She laughed again. 'Why wait when the opportunity presents itself?'

'Those are my thoughts exactly,' he said.

He stepped forward quickly. Before she could react, he bent down and kissed her lightly on the lips.

She gasped and stepped backward. She raised a hand, with the tips of her fingers against her lower lip. Shock almost immediately gave way to amusement in her eyes. 'Max Quinn! That is not at all what I meant, and you know it.'

He gave an exaggerated shrug. 'How was I supposed to know. It sure sounded like an invitation to me.'

She lifted her chin in mock umbrage. 'Mr Quinn, if I decide to extend some kind of invitation to you, you will not have to wonder whether that's what it is.'

He grinned broadly. 'Now that sounds good. May I expect that to happen in the near future?'

She ignored the question. 'Why are you in town? I thought you went to work for Triangle.'

He nodded. 'Cap sent me way off to heck and gone looking for strays. I ended up close enough to town I decided to sleep in the hotel instead of the sage brush.'

She smiled teasingly. 'And will your report to the foreman include that fact?'

'Hadn't planned on it. Hadn't planned on telling him I kissed a pretty lady, either.'

He was rewarded by the repetition of her bright red blush. 'You'd better not!' she exclaimed. 'And don't try it again, either.'

Lines appeared impishly at the corners of his mouth. 'I'll wait till the next chance I get.' He turned suddenly serious. 'I did find out you were right.'

'About what?'

'The fire at Waltman's. The back side of it was

80

soaked in coal oil before it was set on fire. I can still smell it where it ran down on the ground at the back.'

'That's what you were doing back there! Maude McClaussen was in earlier, and she said she thought it was you poking around. Then she said you lay right down on the ground.'

He grinned. 'Word gets around fast.'

'In this town, yes. Did it surprise you the fire had been deliberately set?'

'No. The only other thing that would've started and spread it that fast is if a lamp got upset, and somebody would've noticed that right away. No, somebody sure enough set it.'

'And who that somebody was is just as big a mystery as it was the night of the fire.' The bitterness in her voice crackled like lightning.

'You think it was McMaster.'

'Who else! Anybody who gets in that man's way has an accident, gets killed, supposedly by Indians or "person or persons unknown", gets burned out, bought out or chased out. That's the third saloon competing against him that just happened to burn down, over the past three years.'

'You mean there are other people besides—' He hesitated, fearing he would rouse her grief afresh.

'Besides Fred?' she finished for him. 'Oh, yes! You found Fuzz Slocum, supposedly caught rustling and hanged, by "persons unknown", Bat Westerman had a small place up the valley from us. He froze to death, leaning against a tree, during a blizzard. But his

81

hands and arms were pulled backward around the tree. It was painfully obvious he was tied there and left to freeze, then whoever did it took the ropes off before he was found.'

'Another "person or persons unknown"?'

'Oh, no! That one was ruled accidental death by exposure.'

She went on, as if reciting a well-rehearsed litany. 'Lefty Westhall was shot from ambush. John Stock was supposedly killed by Indians, like Fred was. Al Hartford, a good and honest town marshal, was shot to death from an alley. That one was "person or persons unknown". So was Tuffy Jensen, the marshal between Al and that excuse of a marshal we have now.'

'Quite a list.'

'All of them people in Virgil McMaster's way. The only thing I don't understand is how he decides who needs to be killed.'

'All those people weren't in competition to his business. What's his game?'

She sighed heavily. 'I'm not entirely sure. The whole country is on the verge of going to war against itself, it seems like. It all comes back to him, though. I'm sure of it.'

'Hard to see how one man could be causing that much trouble.'

'He's evil, Max.'

'I'm hungry,' he switched the subject. 'Shall we go eat?'

They crossed the sidewalk and stepped into the

street when the cold voice stopped them in their tracks. 'Max Quinn.'

Max whirled to face the unexpected voice. The man standing in the street was obviously a gunfighter. His stance was tense. His right hand was poised just above the butt of a .45 that had obviously seen a great deal of use.

Dottie's hand flew to her mouth. She made no sound, save a small gasp, quickly stifled. Max pushed against her with his left hand. She understood instantly, and moved away from him, crossing the rest of the way to the far sidewalk. She stopped there, fear etched on her face.

From the corner of his eye, Max spotted Curly Winters, one of the gunmen from the Triangle, lounging against the front of a store across the street. His presence troubled Max, but the one in the street demanded his whole attention.

'Who are you?' Max asked, facing the one who had called out to him.

'Don't matter none,' was all the reply the question evoked. 'I know you from down in Kansas.'

Max frowned. 'I've never been in Kansas.'

'Sure ya have. Salinas. You killed a friend o' mine there.'

'You've got the wrong man, mister. I've been in the Indian Nation, Dakota Territory, Nebraska, Wyoming. That's it.'

'Ain't no good tryin' to weasel out. I knowed ya soon as I laid eyes on ya.'

'Probably not the first thing you've been wrong

about,' Max allowed.

The gunman lifted his left hand toward Max as if to say something further. It was a move intended to distract him from the lightning move of his right hand on his gun butt. Faster than the striking head of a rattlesnake his gun lifted from its holster. The man was good. Fast. Incredibly fast.

Whatever the intent, it and his draw were inadequate. His gun was just coming up from the holster when the .45 in Max's hand barked. The slug slamming into the gunman's heart made his own shot slightly errant. It passed just over Max's left shoulder. He clearly heard the whine of the bullet as it streaked past.

It was probably the sound of that near miss that caused the second blast from the muzzle of Max's .45. It was so instantaneous behind the first shot that its roar blended into the other two, but it was unnecessary. The gunman's heart had already exploded from the impact of the first round.

With his gun still leveled, Max's eyes sought out Curly Winters. He continued to lean indolently against a store front. Surprisingly, Ralph Small emerged almost immediately from his office, gun in hand. He quickly sized up the situation. Holstering his gun, he strode toward Max. 'You again,' he accused.

'Good to see you too, Marshal,' Max said. He made no effort to hide his sarcasm. 'Who's your friend?'

The marshal's watery eyes flashed the barest hint

of fire before they lost their spark again. He glanced at the dead gunman. 'No friend of mine,' he denied.

'Who's he work for?' Max demanded.

The marshal shrugged. 'Danged if I know. Don't recollect seein' 'im afore.'

'Someone sent him to kill me,' Max declared. 'Now just who do you suppose doesn't like me that much?'

'Now that's hard to say. You ain't made too many friends around town,' the marshal declared.

'I didn't know I'd made any enemies, either.'

'You killed a man.'

'I killed a card cheat.'

'He likely had friends. Why'd ya pick a fight with this guy?'

Max's jaw clenched, but he held his voice steady. 'I didn't. Quite a few people on the street heard the whole thing. He called me out. Claimed I killed a friend of his in Kansas. He was wrong: I've never been to Kansas.'

'So you say.'

Max's patience ended instantly. His eyes flashed. He took a step toward the marshal. 'Are you calling me a liar?' he demanded.

The marshal backed down immediately. He lifted both hands, palms outward, toward Max. 'I didn't say nothin' of the kind,' he denied.

Max pressed the issue. 'The man called me out. I killed him in self-defense. Do you have any problem with that?'

Small shook his head vigorously. 'I got no problem

with that. If it wasn't self-defense, some o' these folks woulda said so already.'

'Then I'll let you see to having the body taken care of.'

Max turned on his heel and strode to where Dottie still waited on the sidewalk. He already knew both their appetites and the light mood of the day were long gone. What he didn't know was who had hired a gunman to kill him. Or how many more were lining up for their turn.

CHAPTER 11

Dark foreboding filled the bunkhouse. One cowboy was already asleep, snoring loudly. Two others were nearly ready for bed. Max and Champ lolled on their bunks, talking quietly.

Three of the hands, who were obviously hired only for their guns, were, as usual, busily cleaning and oiling the tools of their trade. Max noted that each kept a second gun ready at hand on the table, while cleaning another one.

Only one of them, Curly Winters, appeared to take any notice of Max's presence. Glancing in Max's direction, he finally spoke. 'I saw you in town the other day,' he accused.

Max's eyebrows lifted slightly, but his expression did not otherwise change. 'Sure did. Lookin' for strays over where Cap sent me. Ended up a little over a mile from town. The hotel sounded like a lot better sleepin' than the ground. It's plumb rocky over there.'

The gunman wasn't willing to leave it at that. 'Someone in town you was wantin' to see?'

The charged atmosphere within the room fairly crackled with tension. Max's voice was softer as he answered. 'Would it be some business of yours if I was?'

The gunman smiled, but there was no mirth in the expression. Max thought suddenly he looked almost as if a forked tongue would snake out between his lips to taste the air at any moment. 'Just wonderin'. Figured you either got a girl in town, or you're takin' orders from someone besides Cap.'

Max eyed the man in the flickering lamplight. 'What do you mean by that?'

'I heard you been gettin' plumb friendly with the Fancher widow.'

'Now where would you hear that?'

He shrugged, but his beady eyes never left Max. 'I got ways of knowin' things. Her old man was one o' the problems around here.'

'What kind of problem?'

'Kept tryin' to organize the small ranchers and homesteaders against the legitimate ranchers. Not a healthy thing to do.'

'Is that why he died unexpectedly?'

The question seemed to have no effect on the gunman. Another of the gunman, however, tittered in a high voice, a falsetto, three syllable giggle, then fell silent. Max glanced at Billy Fugate. The small, almost effeminate gunman's eyes glittered brightly.

Curly spoke. 'The way I heard it, is that he got to wanderin' around over by Inyan Kara. Them Lakota, they don't like white folks bein' over there. Put an arrow in his back, the way I heard it.'

'It doesn't sound like that broke your heart too bad.'

The gunman's smile deepened slightly. 'Probably just saved me the trouble,' he admitted. 'Or Billy.'

Billy tittered again, but didn't speak. It was Curly who said, 'Like I said, he was gettin' to be a real problem.'

'Depends on which side you're looking at it from, I suppose.'

'That's exactly what concerns me. You gettin' friendly with his widow makes me wonder what side you're really on.'

'Why do I have to be on one side or the other? I hired out to ride for Triangle. I ride for Triangle; I do my work; I stay out of the squabbles.'

'It ain't that easy,' the gunman argued. 'Either you ride for the brand, or you don't. If you ain't sure where your loyalty is, you got no business on this spread.'

Max changed tactics abruptly. 'I noticed you in town, too. So I guess I have to wonder the same thing you asked. Who were you in town to see?'

The gunman's attitude changed instantly. 'What d'ya mean by that?'

It was Max's turn to shrug slightly. He used the motion to shift himself so his hand was closer to the butt of his gun. 'Just wonderin'. You didn't seem too anxious to back up another Triangle hand. How long you been ridin' for Marshall?'

'What business is that o' yours?'

Max ignored the question, choosing to press his own instead. 'You been here longer than your side-kicks, ain't you?'

The gunman's gaze was guarded. 'Yeah, I been here nigh on three years. Wes an' Billy ain't been here quite a year. Why? What business is that o' yours?'

'Just thought you might have a better idea where the problems keep coming from between the ranch-ers and the little guys.'

Curly's eyes darted briefly around the room, then instantly back to Max. Every hand in the room was watching the two intently. 'That's obvious, ain't it? The little guys are chippin' away at the big ranches, tryin' to put 'em outa business.'

'More often it's the big ones not likin' the little guys and homesteaders,' Max corrected. 'Other than someone that starts runnin' a long rope, I've never known big ranchers to be too concerned about the little ranches. Except here.'

'Dirt-grubbin' farmers an' homesteaders are always a blight on the land,' Curly insisted. 'I'm wonderin' if they're the ones sent you out here to hire on, find out what we're doin'.'

That was a challenge Max couldn't allow to go unanswered. It drove to the heart of his integrity and honesty. He stood slowly from the bunk. His voice was low, but flat and hard, as if the words were chipped in brittle shards from his mouth. 'Are you callin' me a back-stabber?'

Curly smiled as he rose from his chair. 'Yeah, I guess maybe I am,' he agreed.

Even as he spoke, his hand grabbed the gun that lay just beside it on the table.

He was not all that fast. His gun hadn't quite cleared the table top when the blast from Max's gun drove him backward. He fell past the table where the three had been cleaning their guns, but knocked it over nonetheless. Cleaning rags, ramrods, oil and guns clattered to the floor. Curly's already dead body sprawled among them, his now useless gun locked in the grip of dead fingers.

The other two gunman made a swift show of keeping their hands far from their own guns. Billy's eyes glittered like burning coals, but he was silent.

'Anyone else want to question my honesty?'

The cowboy who had been sleeping stared wide-eyed and confused. The rest shook their heads almost in unison.

'You hadn't oughta done that there,' Billy Fugate said. His words were accentuated by the predictable high-pitched giggle. His hand flirted dangerously close to his own gun butt.

Anger flared in Max. He addressed the slight gunman. 'You wanta try your hand?' he challenged.

Billy giggled again, before answering. 'I just might do that. My time. My place. Not now.'

The door flew open and Cap burst into the room. His eyes made a complete circle of the bunkhouse,

91

taking everything in. 'What's goin' on here?' he demanded.

Before anyone could respond, Champ Haggler spoke up. 'Curly called Max out. He seemed to think Max is a plant, workin' for the homesteaders. He went for his gun first.'

Cap's eyebrows shot up. 'He reached first, and you beat 'im?'

Max's eyes bore into the foreman. 'He wasn't as fast as he thought he was.'

Cap glanced around the room before responding. 'If he drew first, there ain't nothin' I can do about that, I guess. But I won't have feuds goin' on between hands. You can pack up your stuff. I'll draw your time for ya. I'll pay ya for the month, to be fair.'

Champ spoke up. 'Better draw mine too, then.'

Fire flashed briefly in the foreman's eyes, but he held his tongue. His eyes challenged their way around the bunkhouse. 'Anyone else feel that way?'

There was no response. He nodded curtly, turned on his heel, and strode out.

Both Max and Champ quickly put together their bed rolls. By the time Cap returned, both had saddled their horses and stood waiting. 'No need for ya to have to leave with dark comin' on,' Cap almost apologized. 'You're welcome to wait till mornin'.'

Max didn't bother answering. Champ said, 'I reckon we'll be fine. Things' d be a mite chilly in the bunkhouse.'

Cap handed each the money he had coming and

walked away without another word. 'Where you headin'?' Champ queried.

'Town.'

'Figgered as much.'

'You ridin' along?'

'Naw, I guess not. Guess maybe I'll ride over to Deadwood for a day or two. Then I might head over toward Powder River. Get further away from all the gold fever, where a man can punch cows and not worry about all this other stuff.'

Max nodded. 'Things are gettin' a little tense around here, all right.'

'You got intentions with the Fancher widow?'

A look that defied explanation passed swiftly across Max's face and was gone. His answer was slow, thoughtful. 'Don't know, Champ. I'll admit I'm sure gettin' to have a lot of feelings there. She'd make a fine wife, if a guy was ready to settle down.'

'What's keepin' you from it?'

The look passed again, almost like a shadow across his face, for the merest instant. 'We'll just have to see how things play out.'

Champ frowned. 'There something you ain't tellin' me? About how come you're here?'

Max studied his friend a long moment. 'Sometimes a man hadn't oughta show all his cards,' he said. 'Better for everybody.'

Champ started to protest, then thought better of it. He held out a hand. 'Well, take care of yourself, then. Watch your back.'

Max took the hand. The two stood, looking into

each other's eyes for a long moment as the strong grip of each was returned. Both knew without a word being spoken that it might well be the last time they would meet.

CHAPTER 12

It was a short night. By the time he got to town, it was well past midnight. He checked back into the same room at the hotel. With the door propped safely shut, he dropped on to the bed and was asleep almost instantly.

The next day was far more enjoyable. He got a haircut and shave. Then he hung around the barber shop for a couple of hours, just listening to the chatter and gossip of the country.

He stopped by Dottie's store just before noon.

Her eyes lit up as he walked in. 'Why, Max! Back in town so soon?'

'Couldn't see that pretty smile from the Triangle,' he grinned. 'Had to come back to town.'

Her smile broadened. 'Flattery is dangerous. Don't you know that?'

'Why. What's it apt to lead to?'

He was rewarded with the barest hint of a blush. 'That depends on who's flattering whom. And why.'

'Just being honest,' he defended.

'Why are you back in town so soon?' she insisted.

He took a deep breath. 'Cap gave me my time.'

'He fired you? Why on earth would he do that?'

'It seems I had a disagreement with one of his gun hands.'

Her sharp intake of breath telegraphed her instant concern. 'What? Who? Are you all right?'

'I'm fine,' he reassured her.

'What happened?'

'Curly Winters accused me of bein' a back-stabber. Thought I was workin' on the Triangle just so I could keep track of what they're doin'.'

'For whom?'

'He didn't say. Just kept sayin', "the little guys" and "the homesteaders".'

Her lips drew into a hard, straight line. Her voice crackled with bitterness. 'Them and us. It always has to be them and us.'

'Seems that way,' he agreed. 'Anyway, he went for his gun.'

'You killed him?'

He nodded silently.

She took a deep breath. 'Well, that's certainly no loss to the country. But Skinny fired you for it?'

'Skinny didn't: Cap did. Said he wasn't going to have his hands feudin' with each other.'

'Well, I suppose that makes some kind of sense.'

'Champ drew his time too.'

'Where will he go?'

'Said he's going to ride over to Deadwood for a while. Let off some steam. Then he said he'd head toward Powder River country. Several big ranches there and up along Buffalo Crick. He's a good hand. He'll find a job.'

'Somewhere that's not about to explode like a powder keg,' she suggested.

'May I take you to dinner?' he changed the subject.

'I'd love that. But I do have to get right back to the store after we eat. And this evening I have to have supper over at Deborah Darling's house. If I had known you were coming to town, I could have made different arrangements.'

A sudden warm glow spread through him. He hadn't been sure his advances were welcome. Her words clarified her feelings toward him dramatically. 'That's all right,' he offered quickly. 'It looks like I'll be in town for a while.'

'What are you going to do now?' she pursued.

He took a deep breath as he studied her calm, gray eyes. That same shadow passed briefly across his face. 'For the time being, I think I'll just keep my head down and see what's going to happen. I don't want to go to work for someone and find out I'm on the wrong side of things.'

'I'm not sure there is a right side of things any more,' she complained. 'The small ranchers and homesteaders are banding together and importing gunfighters. The big ranchers are hiring their own gunmen. Even the working cowhands are spending more time cleaning guns than tending their saddles. The whole country is ready to kill everybody else, and nobody is sure why.'

'Everybody seems sure "they" are plotting and planning and scheming, but so far I haven't heard one solid reason,' Max agreed.

'That's exactly what Fred kept saying,' Dottie confirmed. 'He knew somebody was following him, but he could never figure out who. He thought somebody wanted our place, but after he was killed, the place just sits there.'

'Nobody offered to buy it from you?'

'Not really. I sold off most of our cattle to open the store, but that's all. Except—'

'Except?' he probed.

'There was a man who stopped by about three weeks after Fred was killed. He offered me a ridiculous price for the place. I almost ran him off with a shotgun.'

A smile brushed the corners of Max's mouth as that picture flashed in his mind. Instead of commenting on that, he pursued the other question. 'You didn't know him?'

'Never saw him before.'

'Cowboy type? Homesteader type?'

'Neither,' she shook her head. 'He looked more like a drummer, or a gambler or something. Drove a buggy. Said he'd stop back the next time he was in the area, just in case I'd changed my mind.'

'That doesn't make a lot of sense,' Max mused.

'It didn't to me either. I almost had a sense that he was making the offer for someone else, but he didn't say so.'

The conversation that continued over their noon meal at the café failed to enlighten him any further. When he left her, she gave the distinct impression of waiting for something. Hoping his instincts were right, he lowered his head and kissed her lightly on the lips. She responded warmly, but broke the kiss off much more quickly than he would have liked. 'Be careful Max,' she said in parting.

He spent the evening at the Good Times. He watched those gambling, but did not join in any of the games. He nursed the same beer the whole evening. It was fairly early when he returned to his hotel room.

He slept soundly until just before midnight. In the minutes just ahead of twelve, his eyes flew open. He grasped the grip of his .45. He sat bolt upright in bed. He had no idea what had wakened him.

Moonlight streamed through the window. Its soft shadows gave the austere room an almost comfortable appearance.

Then he heard it again. The softest of taps, three times in rapid succession, on his door.

He stepped over beside the door, clad in his underwear, gun in hand. With his back tight against the wall, he spoke softly. 'Who's there?'

The voice that responded was barely a whisper. 'It is me. Carlita. Let me in, quickly!'

Frowning, he jerked the chair silently from beneath the doorknob. He turned the knob to indicate its openness, and stepped quickly back along the wall.

The door opened just enough for Carlita to squeeze through, and shut again, swiftly and silently.

Max quickly replaced the chair, ensuring that nobody could follow her into his room. 'What are you doing here?' he whispered.

Her eyes swept up and down, openly appraising him. Her eyes twinkled and danced. 'I knew you would have clean underwear,' she said.

Suddenly aware of his immodesty, he felt awkward. He thought of grabbing his pants and hastily pulling them on. Then he decided that would be more embarrassing than standing there in his underwear.

'Did you now?' he said, finally. It sounded lame, even in his own ears.

She issued a short, delightful giggle. 'Yes, I did,' she assured him. She took a step closer to him. 'I knew when I talked with you before that you were a good man. A clean man. I would not have been so attracted to you, otherwise. It is like there is some kind of a magnet that keeps pulling me toward you. I have not hardly stopped thinking about you since you rescued me. Many of those thoughts are not so nice, even.'

Confusion, embarrassment, excitement and a surging, heady desire competed for primary emotion. Desperate to get off the defensive, he said, 'How did you find out where I'm staying?'

'I wait, and sneak a small look into the register book when the clerk is not watching,' she explained. 'Then I hurry up here to you. It is so terribly forward of me, but I can not help myself, what I feel. Then I was so afraid you would not open the door before somebody saw me. It would be such a terrible thing if somebody saw me coming to your room in the hotel in the middle of the night.'

'Sure wouldn't do much for your reputation, that's for certain,' he agreed. 'That was an awful chance to take. Must be something pretty important that brings you here.'

She stepped closer still. The heady smell of her perfume wafted past his defenses. Not fully aware of what he was doing or why, he laid his gun on the bedside table. She laid a hand on his chest. 'I am so afraid for you, Max.'

'Afraid for me? Why?'

'That man, Marshall, he has decided you are somebody that we have hired to come here and kill his gunmen. He has ordered that his men find you and kill you. I felt that I must come to warn you. I could not stand it, I think, if something happened to you.'

Her closeness and her message swirled in confused circles in his mind. His efforts to sort them out weren't going very well. 'Marshall told Wes and Billy to kill me?'

She nodded. She was almost against him. Her head was tipped back, looking up into his eyes. Her hand brushed lightly across his chest as she spoke. 'Those two and Lyle Kearns too.'

He frowned. 'I don't know Kearns.'

'He is another of the gunfighters the ranchers have brought in for all the trouble. He is from the

Bald Mountain Ranch. Them and that man, Marshall, do everything together.'

Max did know of the Bald Mountain Ranch, and that they were part of the group of big ranches the Triangle was part of. 'What are they planning?'

She shook her head. 'I do not know. I only just found out that they are looking for you, and that they are planning to kill you. You must try to find them when each is alone. I know how much the mighty warrior you are, that you will not have trouble killing one of them at a time. But you must do so quickly, before they have the chance to catch you when they are together. Oh, Max, I so very much do not want anything to happen to you.'

'I ain't too crazy about that myself,' he assured her.

Blood was pounding in his head. He noticed for the first time the dress she was wearing wasn't the coarse material she had worn when riding. The brilliantly colored fabric clung to her body, outlining the most exquisite form he could have imagined.

Her eyes were moist, gazing into his with concern and longing. He tried hard to think of something to say that wouldn't sound awkward and foolish. He leaned his head down to speak, and was instantly aware his lips were only inches from hers.

He didn't know how his arms had gotten around her, but the feel of her soft but muscular body radiated through that arm to every part of his being.

Their lips met as if they had a mind of their own. She pressed the full length of her body against him. Her lips responded instantly and passionately, sending fire piercing through whatever defenses he had left. Years of loneliness sent a tidal wave of desire surging past every rational thought.

He pulled away from her slightly. She reached up and brushed a hand across his jaw. Her fingers toyed with his hair. Her hand behind his head pulled him back toward her waiting, eager lips. Her tongue darted unexpectedly between his lips. The fire building within him soared to fever pitch.

He glanced down at her dress. He knew instantly his mind was playing tricks on him. The garment was no longer the bright colorful patterns of the Spanish skirt. It was pure white. It reflected the ambient moonlight in the room as if it, too, were lit by some raging, inner fire.

Memory of the icy grip of his nightmare rushed back, filling him with sudden irrational dread and fear.

Dottie's face appeared for an instant in his mind, then vanished.

He put his hands on her shoulders, pushing her away gently. It felt strange, foreign, wrong, to be pushing against her when every fiber of his being ached to grasp her to himself in wild abandon.

'Carlita,' he fumbled, 'don't. We, I mean, there isn't, I mean we don't want to do this. I – I don't want to ruin your reputation.'

'Nobody knows I am here,' she whispered urgently. 'I was very careful.'

'I know. I know. But we can't.'

She stepped back. A pretty pout puckered her

mouth. 'You are in love with somebody else?'

'I – I just think we oughta wait. That's all. Not rush into this.'

Her eyes flashed for just an instant, then went warm and moist with desire again.

'You are so beautiful,' he gushed. 'I have never seen a woman as beautiful as you.'

She smiled. She spun around once, flaring her skirt away from her perfectly formed legs. She tipped her head back saucily. 'When you think you are ready for Carlita, Max Quinn, it may be that Carlita will not be ready for you. Or it may be that Carlita will be so hungry for you that you will never be disappointed in a desire again.'

The thought of her walking out of his room, leaving him once again alone, was almost more than he could bear. Fighting the urge to take her back into his arms, he rushed to the door. Silently he jerked the chair from beneath the knob. He opened it, looking both ways up and down the hall.

'You better go,' he said. His voice was husky, trembling. 'Before somebody sees you here.'

'Do not forget to be careful, my wonderful Max,' she said. She brushed the tips of her fingers across his cheek. 'And be sure you take care of those terrible gunmen before they have the chance to hurt you. I could not stand the sorrow if something happened to you.'

She flashed him a dazzling smile that left his knees weak. She reached up and kissed him again. Then she was gone, like some passing shadow across the moon.

104

Relief washed through him as once again he secured the door.

The relief was followed instantly by a profound, aching sense of loss. He looked around the hotel room. It slapped against his mind as more barren and empty than any place he had ever been.

He sat down on the edge of the bed and buried his face in his hands. It was a long time before he fell back into a fitful sleep.

CHAPTER 13

'Do you know anybody that works at the court-house?'

Dottie studied him over the rim of her coffee cup. 'Why ever would you want to know that?'

He sipped his own coffee. 'I need some information. But I need to do it without anyone knowing I'm looking for it.'

She set her cup down. She reached across the table and laid her hands on his. 'Max, you have been so distant today! You haven't said more than a dozen words, unless it was to answer one of the myriad questions I've been asking. I've been trying all day to figure out what's bothering you. What is it?'

The feel of Carlita's body pressed against him, of her full, searching, hungry lips teeming with passion, the delightful sensation of her tongue unexpectedly sliding between his lips, swept across him. It passed, leaving him feeling almost as bereft as her departure from his hotel room had left him. He took a deep breath. 'I need some information.' The evasion sounded hollow, even to his own ears.

Anger flashed briefly in Dottie's calm, gray eyes. 'I'm sorry. I'm asking things that aren't any of my business, I guess.'

The hurt in her voice was unmistakable. He turned his hands over, grasping hers. 'Dottie, there are some things I just can't tell you. Not yet. But I will. I promise. Just as soon as I can.'

He couldn't read her eyes. It was as if his words sparked no reaction at all. She simply stared deeply, probingly, into his.

'Trust me,' he pleaded. 'I'm not doing anything wrong.'

She continued to stare into his eyes for a long moment. Then she took a deep breath. She couldn't hide the pain in her eyes, but she tried. 'Very well,' she conceded. 'But wouldn't it be just as fair to ask you to trust me? At least if you're not just toying with me.'

The words struck him like a blow. He swallowed hard. He couldn't meet her gaze. 'It'd be fair,' he admitted finally, 'but it wouldn't be safe.'

'What is that supposed to mean?'

'That's really all I can say right now.'

It was obvious that didn't satisfy her at all. Nonetheless, she said, 'Sally Magellan works there. She's a very good friend of mine. What do you need?'

'I need to get in to look at the land records, without anyone knowing about it.'

'You mean deeds, land transfers, that sort of thing?'

He nodded wordlessly.

She studied his face for a long while before she responded. 'I'm sure Sally could show you those records. But it's public information, isn't it? What could be the harm in anyone knowing you're looking at it?'

'I think there might be some answers there to a whole lot of questions,' he evaded. 'For right now, I'd rather nobody knows I'm snoopin' into it.'

She waited a long time for the explanation that never came. She sighed heavily. 'I guess that's all you're going to tell me.'

'That's all I can tell you right now,' he apologized again.

She nodded, with more than a hint of anger in the motion. 'I'll talk to Sally. She can't take those books out of the court-house, though. You'll have to go there. And if you don't want to be seen, it will have to be during the night sometime.'

'That's what I had in mind.'

She sighed as if reconciling herself to something less than she wanted. 'Stop by the house in an hour or so. I'll see what I can do.'

Because they were in the café, he made no effort to kiss her. He stood as she did, and waited until she was gone before asking for another cup of coffee.

It was fully dark when he approached her house. He walked across the porch and reached for the door, to knock. It opened before he could touch it.

'Sally is waiting for you now,' Dottie said without preamble. 'She said to come to the alley door, and she will let you in.'

'Thank you,' he said, feeling as if he should be saying a whole lot more, but not knowing what.

'Will you come back here after you find what you're looking for?'

Relief he couldn't explain rushed through him. 'I was sure hopin' I could.'

'Of course you can,' she said. 'I'll be waiting for you.'

He nearly floated to the alley behind the courthouse. He stood in the shadows, watching and listening for several minutes. He couldn't shake the feeling that he was being watched. Try as he might, though, he could neither see nor hear anything. Keeping to the shadows he approached the back door of the darkened building. He knocked softly.

His knuckles barely contacted the door the second time when it was pulled open. 'Step in quickly,' a feminine voice requested.

He slid inside, feeling the door shut instantly behind him.

'Can you see to follow me?' the same voice enquired.

He hesitated, letting his eyes adjust. As soon as he could make out her dim outline, he said, 'Sure.'

She turned to a stairway, ascending silently. He stayed close behind her. In another part of the building he could hear men's muffled voices, but could not discern anything being said.

At the top of the stairs she led him to a door midway along a hallway. She closed the door, then went to the windows and fussed with the draperies, assuring herself they were tightly closed. Only then did she light the kerosene lamp.

The flare of the lamp seemed brilliant in contrast to the darkness to which his eyes had grown accustomed. He blinked several times rapidly.

Sally Magellan was a very attractive woman, possibly thirty-five, he guessed. He was gripped suddenly by the risk to her own reputation she was taking, meeting him alone in the middle of the night. 'I really appreciate your doing this.'

Sally only nodded. 'Dottie told me I could trust you, or I wouldn't be here. What records do you want to see?'

'I'd like to see who's ended up with title to the places that have been vacated over the past two or three years.'

Tight lines appeared abruptly at the corners of her mouth. 'Would it be adequate for me to just tell you?'

He thought about the offer for a long moment. Fearful of hurting her feelings, he said, 'It'd be enough to confirm my suspicions, I 'spect. But for a couple reasons, I really need to see the records for myself.'

She nodded as if he had confirmed something unknown to him. 'Dottie told me you would,' she offered. 'Though she really doesn't understand why you don't trust her.'

'I trust her completely,' he defended, 'but I don't want to put her in any danger.'

'How would your trusting her put her at risk?'

He sighed heavily. 'Ma'am, I can't explain that to you, either. Not now.'

Her cool blue eyes studied him almost without expression for a long moment. Then she turned on her heel and walked into an adjoining room. She returned with a book so large and thick he wondered that she could carry it. She laid it on an empty table and opened it, as if she knew exactly what pages to examine.

'Here's one,' she pointed. 'It's a proven homestead on Spring Creek. The owner disappeared, and was declared dead. A transfer of deed was filed with his signature, showing the place was sold to Virgil McMasters.'

He grunted in response. She started to turn the page, but he held out a hand to stop her. 'Let me write down that location,' he said, making notes on the first of several pieces of paper he had removed from his shirt pocket.

When he finished, he nodded. She turned several pages, and pointed again. 'The owner of this place left the country, even though his ranch seemed to be doing well. Again, it is recorded as having been sold to Virgil McMaster.'

He noted the location and description of the ranch. She turned some more pages. 'This place is just above Dottie's, toward Temple Mountain. The owner ran into some trouble, that nobody really knows much about. All anyone knows is he was beaten up terribly. He sold the place to someone named Winston McAfee, who sold it the next day to

Virgil McMaster.'

Max frowned, noting the information.

When she had pointed out more than a dozen places that had passed into the ownership of Virgil McMaster, he said, 'That's probably plenty. I thank you again for your help.'

'And you found exactly what you knew you'd find?'

He nodded. 'I was pretty sure that's what was going on. I wasn't sure the records would be that plain.'

She hesitated as if uncertain whether to say what she wanted to say. 'Well, you were right to not come in during regular hours and ask to see the records. Two other people have done that in the past five or six months. Leo . . . uh, one of the people who works in this office, left on some errand right after they left, both times. Neither man has been seen in town since. I don't know if that really means anything, but be careful.'

'Thank you,' was all he could think of to respond.

Sally studied him for a long moment. 'Dottie is growing quite fond of you,' she announced abruptly. 'I hope you don't make her lose two men.'

He felt the blood rush to his face. He labored mightily to keep the feelings the announcement triggered from affecting his voice. 'I'll do my best to stay alive,' he assured her.

Without another word she blew out the lamp. The room was thrown into pitch blackness. He heard, rather than saw, her move silently to the windows and open the draperies. Moonlight softened the darkness. As his eyes adjusted, he could once again make out her form. 'I'll show you out,' she said.

He followed her to the outside door and slipped quickly outside. He heard the soft snick of the lock behind him as he hugged the shadows and moved away.

The soft voice from the deep shadows against a building caught him completely by surprise. 'Find what you was lookin' for?'

He stopped dead in his tracks. He strained to hear, but could hear only the pounding of his heart. He studied the shadows. Only when the man spoke again was he able to make out the vague outline of his form in the darkness. 'Odd time o' night to be prowlin' around the court-house,' the voice insisted.

Stalling for time, Max asked, 'Why would that concern you?'

A door in the side of a building opened abruptly. Light spilled out, revealing the man no longer hidden in shadows. Both men were keyed for action. The sudden burst of light served as a trigger equally unexpected to both. Both men whipped guns from their holsters, belching fire and death.

Max felt his hat fly from his head, even as he heard the unmistakable 'thwack' of his bullet striking the other man squarely in the chest. The force of the bullet slammed the man back against the wall behind him. His gun hand sagged downward. He slid slowly down the side of the building. A smear of blood, dark against the raw boards, marked his trail.

A voice from the lighted room demanded, 'What's goin' on out there?'

'It's OK,' Max called back. 'Some guy tried to waylay me here.'

'Did you hit 'im?' was the instant query.

'He's down,' Max replied.

'Want me to get the marshal?'

'That'd be good.'

The door shut, plunging the space between buildings into darkness again. Max used the darkness to move quickly away. 'Let the marshal wonder,' he muttered.

CHAPTER 14

Dottie opened the front door as Max crossed the porch. 'Did you find what you needed?'

'Yeah, I think so. Found more than I expected on the way back.'

'What do you mean?'

'Someone was either watching me, or watching the court-house.'

Her sharp intake of breath betrayed the rush of fear that engulfed her. 'Someone . . . who?'

He shrugged. 'Didn't get to ask his name. He just said I shouldn't be nosin' around in the court-house that way.'

'What happened?'

'He was real deep in shadows. I couldn't even see him. Then someone opened a door, and the light shone right on him. Spooked him. He went for his gun.'

'I heard the shots,' she acknowledged. 'I was afraid it was you. At least he—'

At that point she noticed the ragged tear at the top

of the crown of his hat. 'Oh! Your hat! There's a tear. . . . Was that. . . ?'

He took the hat off and studied it. 'That's how close he came,' he admitted. 'I think he was a mite slow. Anyway, he didn't get a second shot.'

She stunned him by throwing herself into his arms. 'Oh, Max! Do you have to take so many chances?'

Without even thinking about it, he responded by wrapping his arms around her, vitally aware of the feel of her body pressed against him. He buried his face in her hair, inhaling its fragrance, trying to keep his wits about him. He fought to keep his voice steady. 'If he wasn't dead, I'd go thank him.'

She was silent for an instant, but made no effort to move away from him. 'What?'

'If he wasn't dead, I'd go thank him,' he repeated.

'Whatever for?'

'For gettin' you to do this.'

She leaned her head back without releasing her grip around him. 'If you wanted your arms around me, why didn't you just put them there?'

'Scared to,' he admitted. 'I wasn't sure you . . . felt like that.'

'Not very bright, are you?' she teased.

Instead of answering he lowered his face to hers. The fire that immediately surged within him rivaled, or maybe surpassed, that kindled by the passionate kiss of Carlita. Dottie pulled away, then. Self-consciously, she brushed at the front of her blouse. She cleared her throat. 'I think we're getting ahead of ourselves here.

116

We better talk about what you went to the court-house to find,' she offered.

He noted the slight tremor in her voice. It didn't come close to the emptiness he felt as she stepped back away from him. 'There's other things I'd rather talk about,' he suggested.

She shook her head. Struggling against the rush of her own desires, she said, 'Not . . . not now. Not yet. Did you find what you were looking for?'

'I think so. I got some questions though.'

'That I can answer?'

'I'm hopin' so.'

'Well, come on in. I'll pour us some coffee.'

As he sipped the scalding brew, Max scanned the notes he had made. 'The place just up the crick from yours . . . the record says it was sold to Winston McAfee. Do you know him?'

'I knew he was the one who bought it. I had never heard of him. I've never seen him or heard of him since, either. I don't know what he plans to do with the place.'

'He sold it to McMaster.'

'He what?'

'Sold it to McMaster, the day after he bought it.'

Bitterness edged her words with brittle ice. 'That figures.'

'Then there's the Blanchard place. I heard he lost the place in a poker game.'

'Yes, but he would never say who won it from him.'

'The deed shows McMaster owns that place too.'

'Which means he lost it at the Good Times.'

117

He nodded. 'That would seem to be the case. Here's one that's plain as day doesn't jibe. Remember Fuzz Slocum? The guy who was hanged, supposedly for changin' brands on a Triangle steer?'

'I remember. I knew Fuzz. He was a good man.'

'So I've heard. Well, it seems McMaster showed up at the court-house a week later with a deed to Fuzz's ranch, signing the place over to him.'

'With Fuzz's signature on it?'

'It had a signature. Nobody seems to've questioned whether it was really his. The place was just registered into McMaster's name.'

'That's absurd!' she expostulated. 'If he had sold the place, he surely wouldn't have been stealing steers to stock it.'

'How about the homestead on Spring Crick? The owner disappeared, I think.'

'He dropped out of sight right after he supposedly sold the place to someone named Arthur Williams, for about half what it was worth. I'd never heard of him.'

'Is that so? The records show it being sold to McMaster.'

'He's not the one who's bought up most of the places that have been sold,' she declared. 'I've paid particular attention, because I thought he was behind people disappearing suddenly. But almost every place was bought by somebody else. The strange thing is, none of the buyers ever moved on to the place they bought.'

'And most of the buyers don't show up in the

118

court-house,' he explained. 'Either they don't exist in the legal record, or the record shows they sold out to McMaster within a week or two.'

She frowned as she sipped her coffee, studying him over the edge of the cup. 'How is that possible?'

His slight smile implied no humor. 'Old story. He pays other people to do the buying for him, then disappear. Part of them are most likely made up names. Some of them might be the real names of some of his "security force".'

Her lips compressed to a thin line. Half-moon wrinkles at each end of her mouth emphasized her anger. 'So he's buying up half the country at fire sale prices. Or for the price of a bullet.'

He changed the subject abruptly. 'What do you know about Carlita Daniels?'

The angry expression on her face deepened instantly. 'She is, without a doubt, the most totally evil woman I have ever known. She's broken up three marriages that I know of. She's caused more fights than politics. She manipulates people.'

His eyes danced. 'Other than that, she's a nice girl, though, huh?'

'How do you know her?' Dottie demanded.

He instinctively knew better than to tell her of Carlita' s visit to his hotel room. 'I ran into her out by Bear Canyon when I was riding for Triangle. She said her horse had been spooked by a mountain lion, and run off. I caught him for her.'

'And did she reward you properly for your chivalry?'

119

A smile played at the corners of his mouth. 'She did invite me to stop by.'

Dottie snorted. 'I bet she did.'

'She sure is a looker,' he teased.

'If you care about me, I better not catch you doing any looking,' she threatened.

'Can't blame a man for looking.'

'That's what you think.'

He thought it best not to pursue the subject any further.

CHAPTER 15

By habit, he nursed the same warm beer most of the evening.

A steady stream of men came and went at the Good Times saloon and gambling hall. Nearly all, he noted, left with considerably less money than they entered with.

He watched one of the working girls systematically get a young cowboy staggering drunk. She left with him, laughingly supporting him as he reeled, drunkenly, through one of the doors he knew led to the working girls' quarters. She returned alone fifteen minutes later. At her signal, two of McMaster's 'peacekeepers' exited through the same door. They, too, returned in just a few minutes, laughing as though they had just shared a great joke.

On a hunch, Max slipped outside and walked around behind the saloon. After searching for several minutes, he found the young cowboy. He was unconscious in the weeds, thirty feet from the back door of the saloon. Max checked his pockets. They were completely devoid of money.

He left him there. He was determined to confront McMaster. Now there was one more item on the list of things to confront him about. Surely he would show up in his place of business before the night was over.

Returning as if he had just made a trip to the outhouse, he resumed his seat. Nearly an hour later the young cowboy burst in through the back door. His hat was missing. His hair was tousled. He was decidedly unsteady on his feet.

His eyes cast wildly around the saloon until he spotted the young whore he had left with. Pointing an accusing finger at her, he yelled, 'You rolled me, you two-bit whore! I had six months' wages in my pocket. Give it back!'

One of McMaster's men stepped in front of him smoothly. 'Settle down, young fella,' he soothed. 'You're drunk.'

'I'm robbed, is what I am,' the cowboy bellowed back. 'Get outa my way.'

With surprising strength, he shoved the bouncer aside and stumbled toward the woman who had robbed him. 'I want my money back!' he demanded.

Billy Fugate, the strange young gunfighter from the Triangle, stood up from a table. He waved the bouncer away, and addressed the young cowboy. 'Ain't nice callin' ladies names like that,' he said. 'You better apologize to the nice lady.'

'Get outa my way!' the cowboy shouted.

The customary short, falsetto giggle punctuated

Billy's response. 'You want me outa your way, you gotta take me out.'

'You asked for it!' the drunk cowboy yelled, clawing for his gun.

Billy giggled again, hesitating the barest instant, until the cowboy's gun was nearly clear of its holster. Then his own gun swept up in a blur of speed. It barked four times in rapid succession. Each blast from the gun's barrel drove the cowboy back another step. He folded into a crumpled mass in the sawdust.

Strange expressions crossed Billy's face. His gun still pointed at the dead cowboy. For a moment Max thought he would empty his gun into the lifeless body. Instead he giggled the characteristic three syllable giggle softly again, and holstered his gun. He turned to the woman who had rolled the cowboy. 'You owe me one, Betty,' he told her.

He spotted Max. He stared long and hard at him, as if daring him to intervene. Max rose and walked to the dead cowboy. Leaning over, he picked the dead man's gun up from the sawdust. He checked the cylinder. He dropped the gun again. His eyes glared holes through Billy. His voice was flat and hard as a sheer granite face. 'His gun wasn't loaded.'

Billy giggled yet again in response. 'Now that's too bad, ain't it? How was I to know that? He drew on me. I didn't have a choice. I had to defend myself. I was defendin' the lady.'

Max swivelled his hard eyes at McMaster's security men. 'Who emptied this man's gun?'

The one that the cowboy had shoved aside

shrugged his shoulders. 'I did. We always do that if we hafta toss somebody out. Saves 'em comin' back in an' shootin' up the place.'

'You knew his gun was empty, but you didn't say anything,' he accused.

The man merely shrugged again. The exchange was interrupted by the marshal's entrance. 'What's goin' on in here?'

The security man spoke first. 'Drunk cowboy started accusin' one o' the girls of rollin' him. Pulled a gun. Fugate shot 'im.'

The marshal's eyes darted from the security man to Billy to the man on the floor. Max interrupted. 'His gun was empty.'

The marshal seemed to notice his presence for the first time. He glared in obvious anger. 'What are you doin' here?'

Instead of answering, Max responded, 'The cowboy's gun was empty.'

The marshal blinked several times, trying to digest the information and formulate a response. Max pressed the issue. 'The bouncers threw him out, passed out drunk. They emptied his gun. When he came to and came back in, he pulled an empty gun.'

The marshal's eyes swivelled back to the security man. 'That so, Butch?'

The man addressed nodded once. 'We always do that, Marshal. Seems the safe thing to do. Keeps 'em from comin' back in all mad an' hurtin' somebody. 'Course, we had no way o' knowin' he hadn't reloaded it by then.'

'Nobody told me his gun was empty,' Billy defended. His words were once again punctuated by the short high-pitched giggle.

The marshal studied each of the participants in turn. He spat a brown streak into the sawdust on the floor. 'Seems like a clear case o' self-defense to me,' he dismissed the incident. 'Take 'im down to Eli.'

He turned hastily and exited the saloon, looking neither right nor left. Billy Fugate giggled again. He holstered his gun, winked at Betty, and walked out.

Two of McMaster's men picked up the limp body of the hapless cowpoke. They carried him quickly out of the back door. Max was studiously ignored by everyone in his immediate vicinity. He returned to his table, sipping the warm beer and glowering at the room in general. Within minutes the place had returned to its customary activities. Still McMaster made no appearance.

It was after midnight when Max finally gave up waiting. He again slipped out the back door, waiting for his eyes to adjust to the darkness, then moving toward his hotel. A sound in a nearby copse of trees startled him. He whirled, his gun leaping into his hand. He stood stock still, listening. After a few minutes he heard it again. It sounded like a horse, shifting restlessly.

Holstering his gun, he slipped quietly in a half circle, approaching the trees from a direction that insured no light behind him would betray his presence. He moved silently from tree to tree, listening carefully.

He heard the soft jingle of a bit ring as a horse shook its head. He moved cautiously toward the sound. He was almost on top of the black gelding before he spotted him in the deep darkness of the trees. The horse was quietly watching his approach. His eyes took in the Spanish tapaderos that covered the stirrups, the silver conched bridle and decorated saddle. He knew with utter certainty it was Carlita Daniels's horse. Jumbled thoughts tumbled over each other in his head.

Why was the gelding here? Where was Carlita? Why was the horse so carefully hidden? There was no indication that she was in any kind of trouble. Her horse was tethered to a tree, invisible from more than a dozen feet away.

Silently Max backed away, returning by the circuitous route he had used in his approach. When he was back within the shadows of the buildings, he leaned against a wall and tried to think.

Several times he rejected the idea his own mind kept returning to. Against his will, that idea became a cold, bitter certainty in his mind. Finally, almost inaudibly, he breathed, 'Well, one way to find out.'

Moving silently, staying in the deepest shadows, he found a spot with a clear view of the secluded, rear entrance to Virgil McMaster's private quarters. He noted what his subconscious mind had already assessed. The waiting mount was hidden in the closest concealment available to that door.

He waited in silence for more than an hour. He tried to deny the ache that knotted his stomach. He assured himself nothing mattered to him, where Carlita was concerned. He told himself fiercely that she was nothing more than a great threat and danger to him.

Even so, his heart sank to his feet when McMaster's private door opened. Lamplight spilled out, framing the two people who stood there. McMaster wore no shirt. His suspenders hung from his trousers, dangling against his legs.

Carlita's hair was mussed and tangled. Otherwise she could not have been more beautiful. He forced himself to breath slowly, silently. He couldn't hear what McMaster said. Carlita's tinkling laughter responded. She slid a hand along Virgil's jaw. She lifted her face to him and gave him a long, lingering kiss. Her voice drifted on the night's silence, carrying only fragments to Max's ears. '. . . so much more man than Carlita has ever known. . . .'

He could not hear the man's low, rumbling reply, but he clearly saw the hand that caressed her body as she turned away. Humming softly to herself, Carlita strode to the trees where her gelding waited patiently. Minutes later he heard the sound of her riding away.

He could not explain to himself why he felt betrayed as he stumbled his way back to the hotel.

CHAPTER 16

It was not the time of day he expected trouble. It stared him in the face all the same. 'Quinn!'

The single word slapped against the raw wood of Sundance's store fronts. He stopped, just a few steps from the front door of the café where he had just eaten breakfast.

His mind raced. In the middle of the street three men faced him in a half circle.

Billy Fugate leaned forward slightly. His hand looked relaxed, just brushing the butt of his gun. His eyes glittered like hard diamonds. His characteristic three syllable giggle conveyed the delight at another opportunity to kill.

Wes Herman stood about three steps to his right. Max's racing mind tried to remember a time he had heard the Triangle gunman speak. Even the night he was forced to shoot Curly Winters, he couldn't remember the man making a sound.

Three steps to Fugate's left another obvious gunman stood, poised in readiness. The name Lyle

Kearns sprang into Max's mind. It took an instant for him to realize it was the name Carlita had planted. It was Kearns who called his name.

'We heard you was lookin' for us,' Kearns announced.

Trying to look as casual as possible, Max assessed the situation. He had seen Fugate draw and shoot the cowboy in the Good Times. He knew he was lightning quick and deadly. He had never seen either of the other two in action, but it was a safe bet they were good.

He made note of the careful distance they had placed between themselves. Even if he got off the first shot, it would be impossible to move his gun far enough to fire again before the remaining two drew their own guns and fired.

Slim and none, he assessed silently his only two chances of survival.

Aloud he said, 'Why would I be lookin' for you boys?'

'We heard you was supposed to find us one at a time an' kill us.'

Max shook his head slowly. 'Now where'd you hear somethin' like that?' He addressed Kearns. 'I don't even know you.'

'The name Lyle Kearns ring a bell?'

'No, can't say it does,' Max lied. 'Do I know you from somewhere?'

For the first time the man looked uncertain. 'I work for Bald Mountain.'

Max pursed his lips in mock thoughtfulness. 'That

up toward Bear Ridge?'

Kearns nodded. 'That stir your memory some?'

'Nope,' Max assured him. 'I ain't never ridden up that way. Just heard about the ranch. I sure don't know why I'd have any quarrel with you.'

The uncertainty that spread across Kearns's face gave Max his first hope of surviving the confrontation he hadn't invited. Kearns glanced at his two comrades for direction. That timid ray of hope was shattered for Max in the next second.

Wes Herman's voice sounded for the first time. In a low, rumbling growl, deeper than any voice Max had ever heard, he said, 'That's talk enough. We know you're itchin' to have at us, Quinn. So go for your gun.'

Billy Fugate couldn't stifle his giggle. 'Yeah,' he agreed. 'Let's see if you're fast enough to deal with all three of us all by yourself.'

The only hope Max had left was that perhaps their aim would be off. He thought briefly of diving to one side as he drew his gun. He dismissed the thought just as quickly. That would only slow him down and increase the already impossible odds.

He guessed Fugate was the fastest of the three. That further clouded his chances. If he drew and shot the man on either end first, he could swing his gun in one continuous motion toward the other two. Needing to deal with center man first meant he would have to swing his gun one direction, then reverse direction for his third shot. The time required to do that raised the already impossible odds.

Any way he acted, he was a dead man. His only chance was to try to take the three with him, and hope he might somehow survive the wounds he would certainly receive. He had heard of men surviving simultaneous wounds.

Dottie's face passed across his consciousness. He would never have the opportunity he had thought was finally his. His whole life he had dreamed of the day he would find someone that would truly love him, someone with whom he could build a home, raise a family.

Quite by accident, he had found Dottie. They hit it off so perfectly together it was as if they were destined for each other. She even owned that piece of land they could begin with. It was as ideal as if it were a fairy-tale from childhood.

Now it would never be. He would never even get the opportunity to explain to her why he was there. She would never even know who he really was. She would only know she had lost the second man she had loved. 'Don't make her lose two men.' Sally Magellan's words echoed in his memory.

Carlita's sensual form flashed across his mind. As if in a distant dream he heard her say, 'You will not have trouble killing one of them at a time. But you must do so quickly, before they have the chance to catch you when they are together.'

In a flash of insight he knew who had told the three he was planning to kill them. He wasn't sure how she had done so. He only knew that Carlita had staged this situation as carefully as if she were manipulating puppets with strings.

It had certainly worked. He would die here today, and nobody would even suspect her involvement.

Facing certain death enabled the mind to process an impossible amount of information in an instant. As the parade of thoughts and images streaked across his mind, deep despair welled up within him. Everything he had planned and hoped and dreamed would end within the minute, as his blood soaked into the hoof-beaten ground of Sundance's main street.

He tensed to draw, determined at least to die in the midst of the best effort of which he was capable. The echo of Billy Fugate's words, 'Let's see if you're fast enough to deal with all three of us all by yourself' was still bouncing from the store fronts when another voice cut across it.

'He ain't all by himself.'

Four men stiffened in stunned surprise. Max's eyes darted to the far side of the street. The three gunmen tried, almost comically, to look behind themselves without taking their eyes off Max. 'Who's that?' Kearns demanded.

Herman's rumbling growl responded. 'That's Haggler's voice.'

'You got a good ear for voices, Wes,' Champ responded cheerfully from behind the gunmen. 'How are you at shootin' both directions at once?'

'You'd better make that three directions,' Dottie Fancher's voice chimed in.

The three gunmen lost all effort to keep Max in

their field of vision. As one, they whirled toward the female voice. Dottie stood in the door of her shop. She stared at the three gunmen over the twin barrels of a twelve gauge shotgun. 'Three on each side seems a whole lot more even,' her amazingly steady voice declared.

Billy Fugate's face turned pasty white. The other two gunmen looked equally uncomfortable, if less terrified. Lyle Kearns grappled for an avenue of escape. 'You say you ain't gunnin' for us?' he addressed Max.

'I told you that to start with,' Max assured him. 'I got no quarrel with you boys.'

Hastily, Kearns said, 'Then let's just say we made a mistake and we'll be on our way.'

Even the ceaseless Wyoming wind held its breath for a long moment.

'Then beat it,' Max ordered.

The three gunmen nearly stumbled over each other in their haste to comply. They strode away in the direction of the livery barn. Only Billy Fugate turned as they walked away. The daggers his eyes shot at Max made it more than clear that he considered the matter far from over. He would have to be dealt with.

When they were gone, Max crossed the street and confronted Dottie. His voice quivered with unexpected anger. 'Don't you ever stick yourself in a gunfight on my account!' he gritted.

Surprise and pain widened Dottie's eyes. It was replaced immediately by anger equal to his. 'I will stick myself in any gunfight or anywhere else I please if I think I need to, to help the man I love!' she declared.

'I don't need my woman to fight my battles for me.'

'I am not your woman yet.' She bit the words off in brittle shards. 'And if I become your woman, I will expect to stand beside you to deal with whatever comes along. If that means a battle, I sure as sin will fight it with you. If you're not willing to give me that much respect then you can just get on your horse and ride off to somewhere else.'

He looked as if he intended to do exactly that for several seconds. Then he stepped forward, wrapped his arms around her, and kissed her forcefully.

She stiffened in shock momentarily, then responded eagerly. She dropped the shotgun. Both barrels discharged as it hit the board sidewalk, sending buckshot harmlessly into the air. Ignoring the shotgun's blast, she ended the kiss and shoved him away rudely. 'And don't think you can yell at me in public, either!'

Champ Haggler's quiet voice interjected, 'I didn't s'pose he could kiss you in public neither.'

Dottie's face turned beet red. She whirled and disappeared into her store.

Max turned to his friend, grinning. 'I thought you were in Deadwood.'

'I was,' Champ confirmed. 'It sure was dead all right. I thought I'd meander back and see if there was any more action here.'

'Your timing couldn't have been better.'

'It was cuttin' it pretty close,' he complained. 'I'd just put my horse up when I spotted them three.'

'Still headin' for Powder River?'

'Oh, I don't know. Maybe I'll hang around town a few days and see if I can make myself useful again.'

That sounded like the best idea Max had heard for quite a while.

CHAPTER 17

'I thought he'd left town,' Max muttered.

'What?' came from Champ Haggler.

Max frowned. 'I'da sworn I just got a glimpse o' Billy Fugate.'

'Really? Where?'

'Just went around the corner, like he was headin' for somewhere in a hurry.'

'Where do you s'pose that'd be?'

Max pursed his lips thoughtfully. 'I got a hunch. Keep an eye on Dottie for me, will you?'

'Why? What're you gonna do?'

'Just a hunch, but if he's headin' for where I think he is, he'll be goin' somewhere else that I think I'd like to follow.'

'Be careful. He's poison. He likes killin' more'n any man I ever knew.'

'I've sorta noticed that.'

With no further conversation, he set off. He walked half a block down the street, went between two stores and walked quickly to a dense stand of trees.

He shook his head to clear away the emotions that standing there raised, unbidden, within him. It was the exact spot from which he had watched Carlita's after-midnight exit from McMaster's private quarters. The spot provided him an even clearer view of that door than it had at night.

His wait was short. He had been there only a few minutes when Billy Fugate came out. He turned and walked purposefully toward the livery barn.

Max followed, careful to remain out of sight.

Minutes later Billy rode out of town. Max saddled his own horse and followed. He made no effort to keep the gunman in sight. He knew he would surely be spotted if he did so. Instead, he watched from a hidden vantage point until Billy passed out of sight. Then he hurried to another vantage point, where he could again watch and follow.

It was past mid-afternoon when the gunman appeared to have reached his objective. He tied his horse in a low draw. Drawing his rifle from its scabbard, he climbed to the brow of a rocky hill. He settled down behind a cluster of rocks, intent on the area that lay before him.

Max left his own horse further away than he would have preferred. He didn't want to get close enough that the gunman's horse would neigh a greeting, and alert Fugate to his presence. Tethering his own mount, he walked silently to a vantage point fifty feet from the gunfighter. He waited and watched in silence.

Nearly an hour later Fugate tensed. His characteristic giggle carried clearly to Max's hidden location. The gunman removed his hat and rested his rifle across a rock. He waited several minutes, then lowered his head to sight down the rifle's barrel.

Max's voice was quiet. It might just as well have clapped like thunder.

'Target shootin', Billy?'

Fugate jumped as if he had been shot. He spun, spotting Max. The rifle dropped from his hand, his gun appearing as if by magic in the same hand.

Max's gun barked first, driving the slender gunman backward. Billy tried valiantly to raise his gun to return fire, but a second bullet from Max's .45 spoiled that effort as well. The gunman's eyes glared venom for a heartbeat, then went flat and blank. He folded to the ground.

Max called out loudly, 'Over the hill. Who's there?'

'Phil Henry. What's goin' on up there?'

'You were about to be bushwhacked,' Max called out. 'I'm Max Quinn.'

'Max Quinn! You the guy that shot that dealer who was cheatin' me?'

'That's me.'

'Someone was gonna kill me?'

'Had you in his rifle sights.'

'Seems I owe you twice. Who was fixin' to shoot me?'

'Billy Fugate.'

'The runty little gunfighter from Triangle?'

'That's him.'

'You kill 'im?'

'He's dead. I'll go fetch his horse. And mine. I'd appreciate some help loadin' 'im on to his.'

'I'll angle around an' be up there directly.'

Max made the trip to retrieve both horses. When he returned, Phil Henry was standing by his own horse, studying the gunman's body.

'Now why'd he go wantin' to kill me?' he queried.

'Followin' orders,' Max said. His voice sounded harsher than he intended. 'Seems he was workin' for more than one outfit at once.'

'What do you mean?'

Instead of answering, Max shot out a question of his own. 'Phil, I gotta know: how'd you come to be ridin' along here just now?'

Henry's face turned unexpectedly red. He stammered slightly. 'I guess I can ride wherever I take a notion.'

'You can, but you don't usually ride somewhere without a reason.'

'My reasons is my business.'

Max took a deep breath. 'Phil, for a lot of reasons, I got to know the truth. I don't need to remind you that you owe me one.'

'Two,' Phil corrected.

'Then I need you to tell me.'

Phil Henry hesitated a long moment. At last he said, haltingly, 'I – I was supposed to meet someone in them trees.'

'Someone meanin' a woman?'

Phil hesitated again. When Max simply waited,

determined to have his answer, Phil said, 'Look, Quinn, I'm a married man. I got no business havin' truck with another woman. It's just that . . . I don't know. I just. . . . Yeah, I was meetin' a woman. I ain't like that, understand! I don't go lookin' for nothin'. I ain't one o' those guys that's got a wife an' runs off seein' whores too. It's just—'

'It's just that she's so irresistibly beautiful, and it's so hard to believe that she'd fall in love with you like that.'

Phil looked like a child, caught with his hand wrist deep in the cookie jar. 'How'd you know?'

Again, instead of answering, Max stabbed the man in the heart with a one-word question. 'Carlita?'

The instant pallor of Phil's face betrayed the truth whether he admitted it or not. Once again the question seemed torn from him. 'How'd you know?'

'More'n just a lucky guess,' Max said. As much as he tried, he couldn't keep a tinge of the same emotions Phil was feeling from affecting his tone of voice.

'You sayin' I was set up?' Phil demanded.

'That's about the size of it.'

'By her? Why? Why would she want me dead?'

'That's part of what's got everybody in this country set against each other,' Max offered. 'Listen, I got to get back to town. I'll take Fugate's body to Eli Nikila. I ain't gonna tell anyone about you an' Carlita, so your wife don't never need to know. But you do need to get the word to the other small ranchers and homesteaders that the big ranches ain't the problem.

There's a whole lot more to it, but you tell 'em to just cool their heels. Don't let anybody go startin' anything. Will you do that for me?'

'Who are you anyway?' Phil demanded. 'You ain't just some driftin' cowpoke.'

'I'd appreciate it if you'd keep that quiet for a while too.'

Phil stared hard at him for several heartbeats. He took a deep breath. 'Fair enough. I guess I got more reasons to trust you than not to. You gonna put an end to what's goin' on here afore we got ourselves a full-fledged range war?'

'Count on it,' Max promised.

'Good enough for me,' Phil conceded.

With no further word, Max gathered up the reins of Fugate's horse, stepped into his own saddle and rode away, leading the other mount with the dead gunman securely tied to the saddle.

He did not, however, ride directly to town.

Two hours later he reined in. From the edge of the timber, he studied the Double D ranch yard. There was no sign of activity, except a steady tendril of smoke from the kitchen chimney.

Tying the horse that bore the dead gunman to a tree, he rode down the slope into the ranch yard.

'Hello the house,' he called, as he approached.

There was no response until he reined up in front of the house. Just as his feet touched the ground, Carlita bounded out of the front door. Her face was a picture of delighted surprise. 'Max! You have come to see me! Oh, Max I have been so afraid I was too forward and you would think badly of me and not come.'

She launched herself at him, wrapping her arms around him in obvious elation. She tilted her head back, openly awaiting his expected kiss.

When he did not return the passion of her embrace, or accept the invitation to kiss her, her brow pulled down slightly. She stayed where she was, her body pressing enticingly against him. 'Max, my wonderful, handsome Max, is something wrong?'

Steeling himself against the sensations she aroused in him, he said, 'Actually, I wasn't sure I'd find you home.'

'I shouldn't have stayed home,' she said immediately. 'There are some of the cattle that I should be riding to take care of. But I was hoping so much that you might come to see me, that I stayed home. And it is getting so late, I was afraid I was wrong. But now everything is so very fine, because you have come after all. Oh, Max, I am so very glad to see you! And my father and our hired hand will not be home until very late tonight. It is the absolutely perfect time for you to come to see Carlita!'

'I sorta thought you might be ridin' up by Arrowhead Draw.'

She could not hide the sudden stiffening of her body. 'Why would Carlita go riding up there? That is not where the cattle are that I would need to check on.'

'I ran into a fella up there who thought you were going to be there.'

Anger smoldered deep in her eyes, though she did an admirable job of trying to conceal it. 'I do not know what you mean.'

'You didn't ask Phil Henry to meet you there?'

Something inscrutable flashed in her eyes before she regained control. 'I do not hardly know Phil Henry. I know where his ranch is, but him and his wife I do not know.'

She put special emphasis on 'and his wife.'

'Funny,' Max pondered. 'He sure thought you were meeting him there.'

She relaxed her hold on him and stepped back slightly. Her face was a study in confused sincerity. 'It may be that somebody told him that I would be there, that I wished to see him, to get him to be there. But it would be a lie.'

'I wonder what it would take to make a man believe a lie like that.'

She shrugged her. A pretty pout only added to her beauty. 'The only man I would want to meet anywhere would be you, Max. Why do you seem like you are angry with Carlita?'

He ingnored the question. He asked her, 'That day I caught your horse for you.'

'Oh, I remember that day all the time. Max, my rescuer.'

'That's what sorta bothered me. I never could find any cougar tracks in that valley. It sorta looked like you waited for just the right time to send your horse a-runnin', just so I could be the hero that rescued you.'

She frowned in an admirable pretense of confused sincerity. 'What are you saying to Carlita, Max?'

'Just sorta wonderin' how honest your love really is,' Max offered. 'Especially since I would've sworn it was you that I saw comin' outa McMaster's private door the other night.'

She couldn't quite stifle the stunned gasp that slipped through her lips before she regained her composure. Her eyes at once began to flash fire. 'How dare you accuse Carlita of such a terrible thing! And why would you even be where you could have seen such a thing, even if it had been true? Because I have said that I feel love for you, do you think you can sneak around and spy on Carlita? Is that the kind of man you are? And to think, I believed you to be such a wonderful man! Get out, Max Quinn! Get out of my yard! Get off of my land! Get on your horse and go away, and do not ever think you can speak to Carlita again. I hate you, Max Quinn! I hate you! You are a most terrible person that I never, ever want to see again so long as I live!'

She whirled and trounced into the house.

Max mounted his horse and rode hastily from the yard, expecting at any moment that she might begin shooting at him from the house. He knew with absolute certainty that she would not let his accusations rest without retaliation.

CHAPTER 18

'All hell's gonna bust loose if I send this.'

The telegraph operator in Sundance looked askance at Max. Something in Max's eyes changed his demeanor instantly. 'But I'll send it, mind you. That's my job. I'll sure enough send it. I sure will. Yes, sir.'

Max's voice was soft, but its edges were sharp granite. 'I do know Morse code,' he cautioned. 'I'll be listening. Send it exactly as it reads.'

The operator's face paled perceptibly. 'Sure thing. Just like it reads.'

He sat down at the key. His finger began a rhythmic tapping as the message went out along the wire. He started to send the wrong word once, as if to determine whether Max truly did know Morse code. By the third letter of that word, Max interrupted. 'Whoops! Wrong word.'

The operator cringed, made the correction, and sent the rest of the message as written.

When he finished Max paid him for the telegram.

Then he said, 'I'll be where I can watch you, by the way. I'd consider it awfully unfortunate if you were to, say, feel the need to go tell anyone about that telegram. In fact, I think I can guarantee you'd lose your job and spend time in jail if you were to do that.'

The operator's expression betrayed an intent to do exactly that. He swallowed hard several times. 'I get the message,' he stammered finally.

'I'll know exactly where you're headin' if you leave here,' Max repeated. 'The minute I don't see you through that window, I'll figure you're on your way. You won't make it all the way.'

'Y-Y-You got my word. I ain't gonna tell nobody.'

Max nodded once, turned on his heel and left the tiny office.

Across the street, he made a show of talking to Champ Haggler, pointing to the telegraph office as he did so. When he left, Champ leaned against the front wall of the store facing the office, rolled a cigarette and lit it. He made just as great a show of determination to stay right where he was stationed.

Max walked directly to Dottie's Millinery & Lace Goods. There was one customer in the store. He waited until she left, then approached Dottie. She scanned his face anxiously. 'Max, you look like something's terribly wrong.'

He shook his head. 'Things are about to get right,' he disagreed. 'But I do need to talk to you. Could you close the store for a little while?'

Questions tumbled over each other in her changing expressions for several heartbeats, but her voice

146

betrayed no indecision whatever. 'Of course. I'll put a sign on the door.'

She did so, then joined him where he had retreated to the rear of the shop. Dottie had a small table there, with three chairs. They both sat down.

He got right to it at once. 'I got some things I need to tell you,' he said. 'You've been askin' me questions I couldn't answer for a while. I'll tell you what I ain't been tellin' you, then I'll answer any question you got.'

'Am I going to like what I'm about to hear?'

He gazed intently into her eyes. 'I sure hope so. The biggest thing I ain't told you, is that I'm a United States Marshal.'

As he spoke, he laid a US Marshal's badge on the table between them. Her instant response was, 'Oh, thank God! I knew you were hiding something from me, and I've been praying and praying that it wouldn't turn out to be something terrible.'

His heart soared at her response. He continued, however, as if she hadn't said anything, 'There's been a major fear that this area is about to blow up into something like the Johnson County War two years ago. I was sent to snoop around, learn what I could, and figure out how to defuse the situation here without havin' to call in the army again.'

'One man? They sent one man to do that?'

'They sent me,' he confirmed.

'Oh, Max, I'm so proud of you! They must have an awfully lot of confidence in you! But ... what happens now? And what about us? When this is over, will you just ride away to some other job, some other place, some other . . . woman?'

As she finished the sentence, her lower lip quivered.

Max reached out and took her hands in both of his. 'Dottie, unless you make me, I ain't never gonna ride away from here. I wanta stay where you're at for the rest of my life.'

Her eyes abruptly brimmed over with tears. She bit her lower lip to control her emotions and remain silent.

'I've sent a telegram,' he rushed on. 'Things are gonna come to a head tomorrow. After that, if I'm still alive – and I sure intend to be – I got some other things to say to you.'

'What . . . what happens tomorrow?' she asked.

'If you'll let me, I'll keep that to myself for right now. If things work out right, it'll all happen real peaceable.'

'And that's all you can tell me? Even now?'

'Well, I can tell you that your two favorite people in the world are gonna be mighty unhappy.'

Her brow knit in sudden confusion. Then the sarcasm of his calling them her two favorite people registered. Her face cleared as if a cloud suddenly disappeared from across the sun. 'Well, that's good to know at least,' she sighed.

A sudden thought changed her expression. 'Is Champ part of this?'

'He is now,' Max confirmed. 'He wasn't. I let him in on it while ago. I had to, so he'd watch the telegraph operator. I'm sure as anything he'd hightail it straight to McMaster with the message I sent if we let 'im.'

'And the marshal?' she probed.

Max laughed shortly, harshly. 'Not a chance. He's gonna be as surprised as anyone.'

'Oh, Glenda and Wilma will be so happy.'

It was his turn to be confused. 'Who are Glenda and Wilma?'

'Their husbands were both town marshals before Small. They were both killed.'

'By person or persons unknown,' he intoned.

'Oh, Max! You will be careful, won't you?'

He nodded, squeezing her hands. 'I won't be alone this time. The boys I sent for are hell on high red wheels when things start poppin'. Just you keep you an' that shotgun of yours outa sight where you don't get hurt.'

She giggled. He rose from the table. 'I gotta go. Lot of things to get set up.'

She rose as well, gliding into his arms as if it were the most natural thing in the world. She pulled his head down toward her. The kiss she gave him left him with no doubt. He had more than adequate reason to be sure he survived the approaching storm.

CHAPTER 19

'Mind if'n I sit here, Mr Quinn?'

Max raised his eyebrows slightly. His mouth full, he simply waved a hand at the empty chair across the table from him.

The scrawny old man, reeking of stale beer and sweat, sat down hastily. He cast a surreptitious glance around the café.

'Can I buy your breakfast, Scruffy?' Max enquired when he had emptied his mouth of food.

'Why, thank you Mr Quinn. That'd be just right awful nice of you.'

Max turned around, catching the attention of the combination cook and waitress. 'Wanda, would you bring Scruffy a good bait o' breakfast, please?'

Wanda looked askance at Scruffy. It was clear she was less than thrilled to have him in her café. It was equally clear she would not refuse to feed him. 'Sure thing,' was all she said.

She immediately brought Scruffy a steaming cup of coffee. She set a pitcher of cream and a sugar bowl beside him as well, without needing to ask whether he used either.

'Thankee, ma'am,' he muttered.

He put all the cream into his coffee that the cup's volume permitted. Then he spooned in half a dozen spoons of sugar.

'That's pertneart syrup by now,' Max commented.

'Costs all the same,' Scruffy explained. 'Like to get my money's worth.'

Max only smiled tightly, waiting for the town drunk to get around to his reason for being there.

When he had taken a couple gulps of the coffee, Scruffy looked around the café again. Then he leaned forward across the table. His voice took on a definite conspiratorial tone. 'Mr Quinn, you been good to me. Never bad-mouthin' me like most folks. Bought me a meal now'n then. I figger I owe you.'

Max remained silent, waiting.

Scruffy looked around the room again and leaned forward a little farther. Max resisted the urge to draw back from the man's foul odor and worse breath. 'There's somethin' in the air over at the Good Times.'

'Why do you say that?'

'Tense, they is. Tensed up tighter'n a long-tailed cat in a room full o' rockin' chairs. An' all o' McMaster's men is packin' extra guns. They're watchin' that front door like a hawk a-waitin' for a rabbit to move. They're lookin' for somethin', an' loaded for bear. Thought maybe you'd best know that, what with you an' McMaster not bein' the best o' friends an' all.'

Max smiled tightly. 'Something's got them upset, huh?'

'Upset ain't no word for it,' Scruffy confirmed. 'They're primed for trouble. Thought you'd oughta know that.'

Max said, 'Thanks, Scruffy. Enjoy your breakfast.'

He got up from the table, paid for his and Scruffy's breakfast and started for the door. As he stepped out on to the sidewalk, Champ Haggler spoke. He was leaning against the front wall of the café, enjoying a cigarette. 'Fellow on the roof of McMaster's with a rifle. What do you bet you're gonna end up in his sights?'

Max frowned thougtfully. 'Seems likely. Not apt to just shoot me, though. Probably a backup for someone else. Can you get where you can handle him?'

'Way ahead of you,' Champ grinned. 'From the roof of the hotel I'll have him dead to rights. If he points that rifle I can point out the error of his ways real quick.'

'I'll hang around here a few minutes to give you time to get there. Then I'll head toward Dottie's store. That's most likely the way they'll be expectin' me to go.'

Without another word Champ dropped his cigarette. He ground it into the ground with his boot heel and walked away. Max leaned casually against the front wall of the café, as if merely killing time. He watched Champ enter the front door of the hotel, then waited another five minutes to allow him time to reach his destination.

He pushed away from the wall and began walking down the street, rather than staying on the sidewalk. He hadn't gone a hundred feet when someone rushed out of the space between two buildings and called out his name.

'Max Quinn! You got a lot o' nerve, showin' your face in this town.'

Max continued to walk toward the man. 'Who are you?' he asked. 'What are you talkin' about?'

'I'll tell you what I'm talkin' about,' the man spat. 'I'm talkin' about you tryin' to force yourself on the woman I love.'

Max continued to walk. It was evident the man had been drinking, early in the day though it was. 'I don't have any idea what you're talking about. Who are you?'

'My name's Will Summers. Carlita done told me what you tried out there when her pa was gone. I love that woman, Quinn. I aim to marry her. But first I aim to kill you for what you tried to do to her. Go for your gun.'

'You got your lines plumb tangled,' Max soothed. 'I never tried anything with Carlita, and you're only one of at least half a dozen guys that think she's in love with them. You don't by chance own a small ranch do you?'

Will blinked rapidly, trying to get his drink-fogged brain to follow what Max was saying. 'What are you talking about? Yeah, I got a small place. What's that got to do with it?'

'She's using you, Will. Every small rancher she's pretended to be in love with has either ended up dead or run out of the country. She's poison, Will.'

Will's face flared scarlet. 'Don't you say such a thing about my Carlita. Go for your gun, Quinn. Now!'

Max had continued his approach as he talked. He didn't hesitate at all. Instead of drawing his gun, his fist shot out, bearing the weight and considerable strength of his whole body. It connected with the young rancher's chin with the sound of a sledge-hammer on a fence post. Will flew backward, landing spreadeagled in the street.

At almost the same instant there were two rifle shots in rapid succession from the roof tops.

Max stepped back swiftly into what protection the front of the nearest store provided. Gun drawn, he watched up and down the street. When he determined the immediate threats were taken care of, he holstered his gun.

Minutes later Champ emerged from the hotel and joined him. 'Just like you figured,' he confirmed. 'Just when he thought you were going to draw, he got ready to blind-side you with a .30-.30. When I yelled, he thought he'd try for me instead. I sorta shot 'im before he had time to aim good.'

Max pulled a watch from the pocket of his leather vest. 'Two more hours,' he said. 'Let's head for Dottie's and lie low a while.'

'That might be a real good idea,' Champ agreed.

CHAPTER 20

'Right on time,' Max commented.

Dottie and Champ both rushed to his side, staring out the front window of Dottie's store.

Six men, riding two abreast, walked their horses slowly down the main street of Sundance. Three wore full beards. One sported a large mustache. The other two were clean shaven. All wore nearly identical, full-length dusters. Their Stetson hats might have been chosen by the same buyer. All rode with the left hand on the reins, and the right hand inside their coats. All had the same steely-eyed hardness to their faces.

Max stepped out into the street, with Champ half a step behind and to one side. The lead rider immediately reined his horse toward Max. He dismounted, shaking hands silently. Wordlessly he pulled several envelopes from an inside pocket of his long coat and handed them to Max. Max opened them one at a time, scanning each in turn.

He addressed Champ. 'We got the warrants,' he

announced. 'McMaster, Carlita, Herman and the bartender, Al. McMaster on four counts.'

He turned back to the man who had delivered the warrants. 'That's the place right over there. The Good Times. You might send two men around to come in the back door. The other four go in the front. Space yourselves so you've got everyone covered. Champ and I'll be right behind you. You all got Greeners?'

The man nodded. 'Greeners and three sidearms apiece. Enough ammunition to start a war. How you gonna get the innocent folks outa there?'

'I'm not,' Max admitted. 'With enough show of force, I don't think there'll even be any shooting. McMaster's men will put up a fight if they have the upper hand. When they see you boys, I'm bettin' they'll fold their hand in a hurry.'

The man nodded. 'I hope you're right. It could get pretty bloody in there, otherwise.'

He stepped back into the saddle. He said something they couldn't hear. Two of the men wheeled their horses and rode at a trot down the street, disappearing between two buildings. The others wheeled as if in military formation and walked their horses to the hitch rails in front of the Good Times.

With calm precision they strode deliberately into the Good Times. The first pair to enter garnered scarcely a second glance, even as they walked quickly to positions, back to the wall, that commanded a clear field of the interior.

The second pair excited considerably more attention. That attention magnified exponentially when the remaining pair entered through the back door and took up similar positions. Before anyone realized what was happening, all six men whipped open their long coats and lifted their Greeners – the short, double-barreled, twelve gauge shotguns. As they did, other things became starkly visible.

Each wore a .45, tied low on the right hip. Each wore a second .45, butt forward, belt high, on the left hip. Each wore a third in a shoulder holster. Each also wore twin bandoleers of ammunition.

What riveted the attention of every occupant of the saloon and gambling hall, however, was the circular badge with a large star dominating. Each bore the legend: Deputy United States Marshal.

In the instant that all eyes were riveted on the six, Max and Champ strode in swiftly through the front door. They walked directly to the nearest of McMaster's security force. Without preamble Max ordered, 'Go get McMaster. Tell him he's got a peck o' trouble out here.'

The man's face paled. His eyes darted around to the half-dozen who had the entire interior of the place fully covered. He swallowed hard. He nodded as if unable to speak. He scurried toward the door leading to McMaster's quarters.

Ten seconds after he disappeared, he came back. Virgil McMaster strode behind him. A cigar protruded from the corner of his mouth. He leaned forward belligerently, glaring in anger at whatever the security man had told him.

Max instantly commanded his entire attention. 'Virgil McMaster, I am United States Marshal Max Quinn, and you are under arrest for murder, fraud, forgery and grand theft. Put your hands up.'

McMaster's eyes bulged in disbelief. He stared at the marshal's badge, now pinned on Max's vest. He swore viciously.

Even as he did, Al, the bartender whipped a shotgun out from under the bar. He didn't get it clear of the top of the bar before a blast from one of the Greeners drove him back into the mirror behind the bar. It shattered. Bottles of liquor toppled in a cascade of crashing glass and sloshing booze.

Another of McMaster's security men clawed a gun from its holster only to be nearly cut in half by the blast from another of the Greeners.

As if by some unheard signal, every one of the rest of the 'peace-keepers' threw his hands into the air. Customers dived to the floor for safety.

In the abrupt silence, Carlita burst from the door into McMaster's quarters. Her hair was disheveled, some of it hanging across her face. Her blouse was torn. A long scratch stood out red against her olive skin, from her shoulder down to where the tear in the blouse ended.

She pointed at McMaster. 'It is true! It is all true! He has done all those things. And he has made me to do terrible things too, because he said he would kill my father if I did not do everything he has made me to do. He is an animal!'

McMaster's eyes bulged further. His already red

face deepened to nearly purple. He swore and said, 'You filthy pig!'

Swift as lightning his gun was in his hand, barking death. Two bullets caught Carlita full in the chest, catapulting her backward through the door from which she had shouted her betrayal.

McMaster swung the gun toward Max, but the blast from three of the Greeners at once lifted him from his feet and catapulted him backward. He landed against a table, shattering it and sending it skidding out from under him.

Incredibly, he struggled to one elbow and tried to lift his gun, still intent on killing Max before he died.

As Max's gun roared, a neat round hole appeared just above the bridge of McMaster's nose. He flopped backward into the sawdust, oblivious to even his own death.

In the unnatural silence that followed, the leader of the cadre of deputy marshals spoke. 'We ain't doin' very good, Max. All but one of the folks we have warrants for seem to be dead.'

Champ chimed in, 'And I'll bet Wes Herman's already saddled and headin' for parts unknown.'

Skinny Marshall surprised Max, speaking at his elbow. 'If he ain't, he will be as soon as I get home.'

Max turned toward the rancher. 'I didn't see you there, Skinny.'

'I pretty well put things together as soon as I saw you walkin' across the street with that badge on,' Skinny replied, in what almost sounded like an apology. 'We shoulda figgered out a long time ago it was

McMaster stirrin' things up. Him an' that gol-danged Jezebel o' his have kept half the guys in the country gunnin' for each other.'

He turned back toward Haggler. 'By the way, Champ, you got a job on the Triangle any time you want it, an' proud to have you.'

Champ grinned in response, but spoke to Max. 'I 'spect we can take care of convincin' what's left o' McMaster's crew that they ain't got a job no more. I think you got someone plumb anxious to find out you ain't among the dead.'

Without trusting himself to answer, Max headed for the door, and a dream that had been a long time coming.